BLESSED, BOUND AND BROKEN

David Skivington

Fisher King Publishing

Blessed, Bound and Broken

Copyright © David Skivington 2015

ISBN 978-1-910406-26-7

Fisher King Publishing Ltd
The Studio
Arthington Lane
Pool-in-Wharfedale
LS21 1JZ
England

Cover photo with kind permission of Susan Aurinko.

For my Grandparents

Many Thanks

Once again there are too many people to thank!

First and foremost I want to thank God for the inspiring people in my life who have made it possible to actually get this written.

To my amazing wife Bee, I love you so much! Thank you for all the support, ideas, patience and cups of chai. For humouring all my crazy ideas, letting me dream and keeping me grounded.

Mum and Dad, I couldn't have asked for better parents. You are always there for me with limitless love. You taught me to care about this world, and to stand up against injustice. All of the rest of my wonderful family too, for your love and laughter.

The very talented and extremely kind Susan Aurinko. For your time, creativity and encouragement. Thank you for the brilliant cover images on Blessed, Bound and Broken and on Scar Tissue.

Malcolm and Janet for answering my many questions and painstakingly checking over details again and again! Also, Catherine Rubin Kermorgant (author of Servants of the Goddess) for the many details about everyday life of the Joginis. I highly recommend reading her novel too!

A huge thanks to Robert Henshilwood, Thomas Shepherd, Karen Howden, Reuben Hollebon and Pippa White who have each had a hand in shaping the novel from it's messy first outing to the final draft. Thank you for all your suggestions and ideas.

To Auntie Julie for her tireless publicity! Thank you for continually thinking of new ways to promote my work.

To Rick, Sam and Rachel for believing in the story and publishing Blessed, Bound and Broken, and for your patience with all my requests!

Most of all though I would like to say a huge thank you to everyone who takes the time to read Blessed, Bound and Broken. I hope you enjoy the story but that you may also be challenged by the situations it presents for while this is a work of fiction the issues raised are firmly based in fact. Having seen at first hand the work in India supported by Dalit Freedom Network in educating people against illegally dedicating their daughters as temple prostitutes and instead offering them an education and opportunities to make a better life, I ask that you take a few moments to read the charities section at the back of the book and check out and perhaps consider supporting those listed.

There are many more people I could thank but this would become another prologue to the book! All those who are part of my life, thank you.

David

Definition of **Dalit**

noun
(in the traditional Indian caste system)
a member of the lowest caste. See also
untouchable, scheduled caste.

Origin:
via Hindi from Sanskrit *dalita* 'oppressed'

Definition of **Devadasi**

noun
a hereditary female dancer in a Hindu temple

from Sanskrit *devadāsī*, literally 'female
servant of a god'

Oxford Dictionaries

Prologue

Flames danced playfully from numerous open fires, leaping and diving as they bathed their attendants in a flickering orange glow. As their smoke drifted into the night sky the smell of charred wood mingled with incense, cooking spices and sweat as thousands of villagers jostled for position in the ever-growing crowd. Some were content to swap stories with old friends by the fire, while others pushed through, eager to bring their sacrifices to the goddess. The night was alive, filled with the sound of animals bleating and squawking; the pious chant of prayers blaring through the speaker system; bursts of laughter and drunken shouting; vendors hawking their wares in husky voices. A cacophony of noise, every sound clamouring to be heard above the others. But the rhythm of the duppa drums rose above the rest of the din. They were a constant presence, steady and ancient; the heartbeat of the night.

It was the first evening of the annual festival, known locally as the Jatara. Despite the tragic events of yesterday it still looked like being the biggest in history, as promised by Giri Kalluri, the Chief Minister for the state of Andhra Pradesh. Rumours had spread that he was going to make a big announcement tonight and people had flocked to listen, speculating on what it could be. His public appearances had been few and far between recently, but with the upcoming elections he was eager to speak to the people and attempt to reassert his authority which was rapidly slipping away.

His words would have to be wise and well considered if they were to have a calming influence. The entire state was currently in turmoil. Recent months had given rise to mass protests in the streets, many turning bloody as people fought to make their views heard. There was talk in the air of a new state being created; Telangana. Some saw this as the opportunity to finally break free from the current oppression and corruption; a chance to start again. In the recent frenzied protests it had been built up by some of the lower castes into almost a utopian state; the more they were silenced with force, the stronger the dream grew of separation from Andhra Pradesh and its leaders. The higher castes had governed for as long as anyone remembered, but many Dalits hoped that Telangana could signal a change, for once an opportunity to select people to represent them and their interests.

However, Dalit neighbours were pitted against each other. Some dreamt of a glorious revolution while others merely wanted to avoid conflict, fearful of the repercussions from the recent violent outbursts. Regardless of their views, everyone was intrigued to hear what Kalluri would say. The winds of change were blowing and they wondered if he would fight progress or find a way to embrace it. All conversations were turned towards politics; many speaking in hushed tones while others spoke out proudly, daring anyone to challenge them as alcohol fuelled their bravado.

Aside from politics, chatter inevitably turned to the horrendous events of yesterday. Those who had been present reported back to the new arrivals, embellishing facts or completely discarding them in their eagerness to tell their own version of the tragedy. Opinions were polarised, the event twisted to justify or condemn those involved. Despite the tangible tension, people still seemed determined to enjoy every moment, wholeheartedly giving themselves over to the age-old rituals of the Jatara.

As always at this time of year the entire village was decorated with bursts of colour. Strings with flags of orange, green and white zigzagged between trees and makeshift poles that were encased in hundreds of electrical wires. Bright lights wound their way around tree trunks, humming loudly as the electricity ebbed and flowed. The white-washed walls of the higher caste houses leading into the village were covered in bright religious symbols sketched in chalk or bright paint.

Many devotees had garlands of orange and yellow carnations hanging around their necks and the dusty ground was painted with swirls of colour, numerous patterns and symbols marking every footstep. Everyone wore their finest attire, with saris all the colours of the rainbow swirling as women danced and swayed. Men were in brand new white shirts and dhotis, starched and clean. Others wore suit trousers and shoes that kicked up the dirt as they moved.

Although it was past midnight, many pilgrims were still arriving from all over Andhra Pradesh to join the revelry and celebrate. The throng now stretched miles back from the temple as people pressed close together not wanting to miss any of the merriment. Bullock carts heaved and strained as they wound through the village loaded with food and offerings for the goddess Yellamma, their owners trudging barefoot with sleepy children slung over their shoulders. Others almost ran in excitement as they neared their destination, the long journey only serving to build their anticipation as they saw the celebrations unfolding before them.

In the centre of it all the Yellamma temple proudly stood like an ornate wedding cake, rising tier upon tier as it stretched up to touch the sky. Layers of orange, red and yellow rose in a tower which was topped with a ringing bell and a red flag flapping gently in the breeze. Strings covered in orange carnations flowed from its summit to the ground as devotees swarmed in and out like bees to their hive, each bringing their gifts of devotion and leaving with a blessing uttered by a bare-chested priest.

Leaning against the temple walls were numerous stalls made from bamboo poles and sheets, created specifically to meet the needs of the travellers attending the Jatara. Some held golden trinkets and souvenirs as reminders of their journey. Others sold animals for sacrifice to help appease the goddess. The most popular though were those selling food to those pilgrims weary from their journey. Cauldrons of oil bubbled merrily away as expert hands created orange squiggles of jalebi and folded sumptuous samosas. Others doled out ladles of rice and dhal onto banana leaves which were quickly consumed.

The crowd was so tightly packed it seemed to move as a single organism, swallowing up anyone swimming against the tide and continuing to build as the night progressed. Thousands had come and thousands more were on their way.

The swell around the temple was greatest, with devotees pressing forward to worship after their long journeys. On arrival they were ushered through the gates by the priests and groups of stern police, then told to circle the temple in a clockwise direction as their offerings were received. Outside the temple gates lay a mound of sandals and shoes, removed as a sign of reverence to the goddess.

The drums were ceaseless as small groups of older Devadasis danced through the crowd, throwing their arms in the air as they balanced crudely decorated yellow pots on their heads cushioned only by thin scarves. They wailed and stamped their feet to the delight of the onlookers. All were marked out by yellow streaks across their foreheads with a large red bindi dotted in the centre of the streaks. Many carried bunches of neem leaves which they waved around, using them intermittently to strike themselves on the back.

The shells on the Devadasi's ceremonial necklaces bounced and swayed as they moved to the rhythm of the drums. If any of the ladies began to tire, one of the crowd would push a clear plastic bottle to her lips to lift their energy. Some men grabbed and pulled at them, but they continued undeterred, their eyes glazed as they stared into the distance. A few men threw rupee coins at them and stuffed money into the folds of their saris while others placed notes into the pots atop their heads. Groups of men circled the Devadasis, many staggering from alcohol as they threw their hands in the air and pumped their shoulders in time to the drums. Some beat their own homemade drums with sticks or the palms of their hands, stamping their feet to the rhythm of the beat. They were often accompanied by others with instruments they had created, sporting one, two or three strings that they strummed as they chanted songs to anyone listening.

Amid the mayhem a silver-haired man stumbled through the crowd, his white shirt soaked with blood. He was shouting and pushing as he made his way to the temple, the crowd backing away and pointing, crying out as they saw him. Emerging through the multitude of devotees waiting to present their offerings he climbed the temple steps towards the cross-legged priest whose voice was resonating through the crowd with prayers chanted down the crackly microphone. Grabbing it from the priest, the silver-haired man began to shout in a shaky voice, "Listen, listen to me all of you!" Some of the chattering stopped as people nearby looked up intrigued, but most continued talking loudly as they jostled to see what was happening. Feedback from the microphone screeched out and people covered their ears, shouting angrily.

"Shut up and listen!" he shouted again as the feedback died out. "Chief Minister Kalluri is *dead*!" he screamed, spittle flying from his lips as the veins in his neck bulged. Immediately the drums ceased.

Silence fell over the stunned crowd as they tried to take in what had been said. He turned and quickly strode to the highest step of the temple, being sure he could be seen by everyone. All eyes were watching him now, mouths open as he paused to be sure of their full attention.

"I was with him. I tried to save him," he said, motioning to his shirt as his voice cracked. He took a moment to compose himself. "I saw it all happen. There was a whole gang of them, ten, maybe more. They were laughing as they did it, saying they were in charge now. They said that they will stop at nothing until *they* have the power." Animated discussion broke out as fingers of blame were pointed and heated words exchanged. Old resentments quickly resurfaced as accusations were thrown between different parties, each quick to blame the other.

"Quiet. *Quiet!*" His shrill voice cut through the rumblings. "You want to know who did it?" He raised a finger and jabbed it towards a field near the back of the temple. "It was those *dirty* Dalit dogs!" he screamed at the top of his voice, taking time to enunciate each word. His eyes darted around wildly as he spoke, making sure he was being understood. "We must not stand for this! If we do, we will all be next!" He drove his fist into his palm, illustrating his point.

An outraged roar bellowed from the crowd. Immediately people began shouting, waving their hands and shaking fists. The fury was easily passed between people in such a confined atmosphere, everyone pushing and shoving with nowhere to go. Someone stumbled and knocked over a cooking pot, sending the boiling contents flying onto those surrounding it. Those scalded retaliated, some grabbing sticks from the fire and brandishing them as weapons. Others quickly copied, pushing over pots and snatching up the burning sticks from below. Blazing torches were held in the air as curses were yelled.

The crowd surged forward towards the temple, trampling anything and anyone underfoot in their frenzied excitement. Entire flower and sweet stalls were demolished, swept along like debris in a tsunami. The stalls crumpled, bamboo sticks falling into the crowd as plumes of coloured spice were dispersed into the air. The man in the bloodied shirt continued to scream into the microphone, but now he was drowned out by the excited cries of the mob. Their anger was fuelled by alcohol and centuries of mistrust and hatred.

The Dalits who had mostly been gathered in a field near the back of the temple turned to flee, but such was the multitude of the crowd surrounding them that they were penned in, unable to move, let alone run. Insults rained down on the Dalits as they were punched, kicked and spat upon. Rocks and burning sticks were thrown indiscriminately, the crowd so close together that the flames easily caught on flowing saris and shirts as desperate screams filled the air.

People climbed the dry and brittle banyan tree standing proudly in the centre of the field, snapping off its branches to use as weapons. Some used it to try and escape, hoping that scaling its branches would provide safety, but within minutes the whole tree had gone up like a giant stack of kindling, its dried arms crackling, and falling down into the crowd below. People screamed as they became trapped in its fiery heights, terrified, desperately leaping from its branches as the flames engulfed them.

Throughout the crowd people clambered over each other to escape the numerous small blazes that were appearing and spreading rapidly. The very ground was catching alight as the spilt pots of oil caught fire sending a streak of flames through the crowd, dividing petrified children from their parents. People used their hands to try and beat out the flames leaping up their bodies while others kicked those who had fallen to the ground. The air was full of anger and fear.

In the middle of the crowd the temple had caught fire too. The flimsy stalls burned up the sides of its walls, with flowers and decorations smouldering on the temple's roof. Smoke poured out as sections of the roof began to crumble, the flames from within licking up towards the night sky. The heat was immense as the doors collapsed, everyone fighting to escape and get away from the temple which had become a furnace.

The electric lights by the temple fizzled and sparked like a firework before shattering as their bulbs exploded, spraying glass onto the ground. All electricity went off, leaving the glowing patches of flame as the only light to view the unfolding madness.

The man with the silver hair hauled himself through the crowd, collapsing on the ground a few hundred yards from the burning temple as he gasped for breath. His bloodied shirt was now also torn and he had a bruise forming on his cheek where a stray rock had caught him. Grimacing, he pushed himself up onto his elbows and surveyed the carnage before him.

As the flames illuminated his face a slight smile played on his lips.

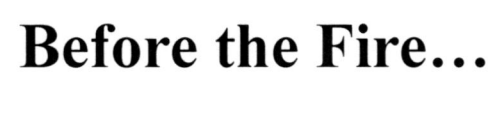

Before the Fire…

Chapter 1

Rupa

As the battered red and green van bounded along a narrow track in the hills, small stones leapt up to chip the already worn paintwork. The van was surrounded by a cloud of dust so thick that Stuart had not even seen the auto rickshaw speeding towards them until its horn blared and he had swerved hard to avoid it, rattling into a huge pothole as a loud bang came from under them. Rupa cursed in the back as she was thrown from her seat, narrowly managing to hold onto the camera as the van stopped abruptly. Stuart grimaced knowing what was coming.

"Stuart!" she yelled. "What have you done *now*?"

"I'm sorry, but you did tell me to hurry. I can't see a thing in here with all that dust and the little scooter came out of nowhere. I bet he didn't even..."

"Just shut up and get us back on the road, we should be there by now!" she said, running her fingers through her hair nervously. "It's already been too long. We can't be late. They can't have done it already." Stuart leapt from the van to gauge the damage, slamming the door behind him.

"We should have called ahead and asked them to wait for us, although it's not like anything is ever on time in India is it?" Ben said, chuckling to himself.

"Is this all a big joke to you? We may have the chance to save that girl's life and you sit here making stupid remarks. Has none of this meant anything to you?" Rupa practically screamed at him. Ben clenched his teeth to prevent him saying something he would regret. He pulled his cap over his shaggy hair and sank down in his seat. He had worked with Rupa long enough to know when a storm was coming and he didn't want to get caught in one now. Who knew how long they would be cooped up after Stuart's latest mishap? Crossing his arms he mumbled an apology and stared out of the window, leaving Rupa to fume in the back. He didn't need this grief. She had been in his face the last few days and he was starting to get pretty tired of it.

A few moments later Stuart clambered back in, his shirt black with oil, cheeks red with shame as he avoided Rupa's eyes. "All's fine," he muttered, wiping an arm across his forehead. As soon as he started the engine though it was very clear that all was very far from fine. The van sounded like a small aircraft and lurched unsteadily from side to side as they crept out of the pothole. "Just need to give it a minute to warm up and..." Stuart began, before Rupa held up a hand, silencing him. He opened his mouth to apologise, but Ben mimed a zipping action across his mouth so he decided to stay quiet and keep his eyes fixed glumly on the road.

They hadn't travelled far, but for the whole journey there had been nothing resembling a smooth road. Every turn was full of craters waiting to rip away the bottom of the van and round every corner there seemed to be a stray sheep or goat blocking the way. Stuart's adrenalin had worn off and once or twice he had felt himself beginning to doze in the hazy sunshine streaming through the window with the van drifting far too close to the ditches lining the road. A decrepit bus lying on its side had helped him shake off his lethargy and Agnipatnam Village was almost in sight now. They had just passed the larger village of Venapalli sitting proudly at the top of the hill, and had been told that Agnipatnam was only a matter of miles from there.

As they rounded the corner to begin their descent they could see the village stretching out below them in the valley. On one side a forest stretched up into the hills but the rest was surrounded by cotton fields which were shrivelled in the summer heat. From this height it was possible to see people milling around through the streets, all heading to a spot behind the temple. A massive crowd was gathered there already, and more were arriving from every direction.

"I guess that's where we are heading for," Ben said, pointing a finger to the crowd. Rupa leaned forward, peering over his shoulder.

"Must be. If there is still a crowd it might not have happened yet, maybe we can still make it. Hurry Stuart."

He nodded, putting his foot down, which increased the rattling from below. He was glad they were headed downhill; there was no way they could have made it up a slope in this condition.

They flew round the corners avoiding any more collisions before coming to the plain at the bottom of the hill. The village spread out before them as they raced along, the streets void of life except for several chickens which darted in and out of small mud huts similar to those they had just seen earlier near the brick kiln. The hut walls were cracked, some with piles of blackened wood outside from burned out fires. Occasionally a pair of scared eyes would peer out at them from inside, but mostly the huts were empty. This was the Dalit wada, the section of the village where the Dalits lived, although most were now at the other end of the village for the hearing.

As they travelled through the village, the housing changed from the simple huts to sturdier brick buildings, many of them white-washed as they entered the higher caste area. Most had gates daubed in neon colours with signs which Stuart now recognised as religious symbols from their previous travels. Numerous trucks rested at the sides of the road, garish scenes from Bollywood movies or 'horn please' scrawled on the back of them.

As they bounded along, Stuart grimaced every time the van jolted, stealing a quick look at the flushed face of Rupa in the rear-view mirror. This was the second assignment they had been on together, the first was in Somalia. The team had been much bigger that time, but now it was just the three of them: Ben on camera, Stuart on sound and Rupa presenting. Things had got pretty gruesome at times in Somalia, but he had never seen Rupa like this. Normally unshakeable, the previous few days had taken their toll and she was all over the place. The last interview they had shot for the documentary had really gotten under her skin and as soon as they had finished she had ordered them into the van to drive to Agnipatnam to try and save this girl. In Stuart's opinion though there was nothing they could do, and even if there was, they were just there to report, not to intervene. That had been made clear to them time and time again. Anything more and things start to get messy.

Stuart had started about five years after Rupa, but he had heard rumours about her first trip to Mali and those lines getting blurred. Details had been hazy, but Ben had been spouting about it when they went for a drink before they set off for India. If anything was going on, Ben was the first to know, even though he had only started last year straight after University. He had a big mouth and revelled in any gossip, trying to pass it on to Stuart even though Stuart wasn't too fussed what others were up to. He preferred to just stay out of it all, keep his head down and get the job done. He had too much respect for Rupa after their time filming together to go gossiping behind her back. Anyone who could travel a thousand miles down a dirt road through a battle zone, see the truck in front blown sky high then appear on camera fairly unshaken was more than worthy of his respect.

He had repeatedly told Ben she was the right choice to lead them, but seeing the way she had been reacting recently he was getting pretty worried. Small chinks were appearing in her usually impenetrable armour. He hoped they were just superficial and normal service would soon be resumed.

Stuart looked over at Ben who motioned with his eyes to Rupa in the back, raising his eyebrows to show that he thought his character assassination of her was justified. She sat with her earphones in, replaying their interviews and growing more and more agitated with each moment.

She was completely absorbed, focusing only on the screen before her. This was the latest interview they had managed to attain and by far the most honest. As soon as they'd start filming, most of the women would immediately clam up, disappearing behind the safety of their scarves. The sight of such technology scared them, and asking them to share such private details with two white men filming them was nigh on impossible. Even more stifling were the unspoken threats in the eyes of the men from the village as they watched. To say too much could cost them dearly, so Rupa had to gently try and coax out any details she possibly could.

Growing up in a Telugu speaking home presented her with a massive advantage. Unlike many of her trips, she was able to work without a translator, meaning she could quickly build rapport with the women. Even so, all she had received so far were grumbles about too much work and the poor harvests this year. Not exactly compelling global viewing for a documentary. She needed something which would show the reality of the women here, an honest account of the oppression of the Dalit women in India. That was what she had promised the producers, but it was proving far trickier than she had initially thought. It was in this interview though that she may have found the first snapshot that began to show life behind closed doors.

A chance encounter with Mounika in the silent brick yard had meant they could film inside her hut away from prying eyes. She still spoke in hushed tones, her eyes flitting towards the door every few moments. Rupa fast-forwarded the initial small talk, cutting to the part where they began speaking about her job.

"How long have you worked as a brick-maker?" Rupa asked from off screen. Mounika fiddled with the filthy yellow scarf over her head and shifted uncomfortably, not looking at the camera.

"Since I was ten. Seventeen years." The woman before them looked far older than her twenty-seven years, her skin dark and wrinkled and her back slightly hunched. She looked momentarily at the camera and Ben zoomed in to capture her haunted expression.

"Did you ever go to school?" Mounika shook her head, creasing her brow.

"No-one in my family has been to school. We are brick-makers. We need no school to show us how to make bricks. What can we learn there to help us? What can they teach my children?" she asked, looking at Rupa for an answer.

They had seen the children on the way into the brick yard. A group of six or seven sat in the dirt, the oldest around eight years of age. They wore only underpants, but these were so dusty it was impossible to tell their original colour. They threw stones in the air among a pile of crumbled reject bricks. All had the same wild, matted hair which looked almost blonde from the constant sun and dust that washed it daily, as well as from malnutrition, leaving it as lifeless as straw.

"What do the children do all day with no school?" Mounika had looked at her as if she was answering a child.

"They sit. They watch. When they are strong enough they help make the bricks. Older ones help make the fire for dinner and boil the water."

"And what about you? Did you ever have dreams of doing anything else?" Mounika shook her head and looked down at her weathered hands, the skin cracked and bleeding around her thumb nail. "We make the bricks," she answered firmly.

"What else could I do?"

Rupa waited though and let the question hang in the air. "There was one time," Mounika began unsteadily, looking into Rupa's eyes. Rupa smiled gently and nodded. "A rich lady came from town to open the new part of the brickyard. She wore jewellery and a gold and green sari." Her eyes sparkled at the memory and for a moment the years of harshness were stripped back, revealing a vulnerable child. "She had a red rose in her hair and looked so pretty. For that afternoon I dreamed of being her. I dreamed of being rich and beautiful." A shout from outside brought her back to reality. She shrugged as a cloud crossed her face and her brow knitted together. "Now I just work. Dreams don't fill the bellies of your children. The boss gets angry at dreamers."

"Tell me about your boss." Immediately Mounika's eyes went to the door. She shook her head.

"Does he hurt you Mounika?" She rubbed her arm absently.

"Only when we work too slowly. If we do not make enough bricks or if they crumble after they have been in the fire, then he beats us or does not give us our pay. It makes us work harder," she recited, no doubt a lie they had been taught to repeat like parrots.

"And what happens if you do not get paid?" Mounika shrugged.

"Then we do not eat. What can we do? Some days all we have is enough rice for one person shared between the whole family. My husband takes first so he has the energy to work, then the children, my oldest boy first, down to the youngest. If there is any left, I eat to stop the pain in my belly."

"There's nothing else that you can do?" Rupa pried.

"What can we do? We cannot borrow from our neighbours. If we borrow from the boss we have to pay it back many times over." Mounika opened her mouth then closed it, unsure of whether to go on. Rupa leaned forward, encouraging her.

"Many of us have borrowed in the past. Every day we have to try and pay it off but the debt only seems to get bigger no matter how hard we try." She looked away from Rupa, unable to meet her eye. "A few of the younger girls, the boss will *visit*. He waits until the rains have come and there has been no work or pay for days. The children get so hungry, you do not know what to do." Mounika sighed and pulled her scarf tighter. "He says that if they please him on his visit it will help reduce the debt, but it never does. If you refuse, he will strike you or throw your whole family out from the brick factory. We have no choice."

"Has he ever visited you?" Rupa asked.

Footsteps outside the hut made Mounika fall silent, her face like that of a naughty child caught stealing chocolate. A moment later the sickly sweet aroma of alcohol filled the hut as her husband entered. He pushed past Stuart and glared at the camera, his eyes red and angry. He began to shout at Mounika in a dialect that was hard to decipher, but she answered back in a curt tone and he looked at Rupa, grabbed a pouch of tobacco and stalked out.

"He says I bring shame being alone with these men," she said, her eyes flicking to Ben and Stuart as obvious foreigners. "He says I should not be speaking to you, but I told him that you would help us for my stories. I told him he just drinks our money so unless he brings me some rupees he can be quiet." It was against the company's rules to pay for stories, but Rupa nodded to Stuart and he grabbed five one hundred rupee notes and passed them to her. She eagerly nodded thanks and tucked them inside her sari, looking at the door as she did so.

"Times have been much harder recently. We have not worked for two days because they have closed the factory. The boss is angry and we are down to the last of the dhal," Mounika stated, nodding to the small pan with a handful of lentils boiling in it.

"Why? What's changed?" Mounika let out a deep sigh.

"Last week a Dalit girl in Agnipatnam was caught trying to seduce a high-caste boy. Apparently she tried to force herself on him. Can you imagine the shame of her parents? How could you raise a daughter like that?" Mounika tutted through her teeth. "The girl will meet with the Shalishi Sabha." Rupa frowned, unaware of the words.

"What's the Shalishi Sabha?"

"When the village elders want to make decisions and they can't wait for the courts to give the punishments, then they do it themselves. Sometimes you wait for years to know what will happen with the courts but with them it is immediate. They will decide what happens to the girl. Maybe she will be hanged," she said matter-of-factly.

"How old is she?" Rupa asked after a moment, her speech thick.

"Fourteen, maybe fifteen, I only know what my husband tells me."

"When will they decide?"

"As soon as they can, the politicians see this as very important, especially with the elections coming up. They want to show the higher castes they still hold the power and can be trusted with their vote. Most likely the decision will be made tomorrow. The sooner it's done the sooner our factory will be open and we can eat again."

"Why does this affect your factory?" Rupa had asked, her head spinning as she thought of the poor girl.

"We are in the same district. Someone decided it would teach us a lesson. We awoke two days ago to find the gates barred and the furnaces put out. What are we to do now? If I could I would hang her myself," she said, eyes looking straight at the camera.

Rupa pressed the stop button and looked through the filthy windscreen. The roads were now lined with people all making the same journey as they were, towards the trial being held by the Shalishi Sabha court of village elders. She leaned forward, straining her eyes to see what was up ahead.

It shouldn't be far now, she thought. If they could get there with the cameras to tell the world, surely they would have no choice but to let the girl go?

She closed her eyes and mouthed a quiet prayer that they could stop it, but as they navigated their way through the crowd towards the court she feared it was going to be too little, too late.

Chapter 2

Mansa

Mansa leaned over the wooden railings listening to the whirr of the printing machines while she waited for Jasmine to bring her more T-shirts. She wiped the sweat from her brow and pushed her damp hair behind her ears, cracking her neck as she did so. It was tough work but it felt good. Her hands were blistered and stained with various colours of ink, but she took pride in what they now did.

She was printing onto T-shirts and could read all of the names she pressed. It hadn't been easy, but day by day the swirls and circles changed from being a frustrating mystery to actual letters that spelt the names of the girls in the factory. It felt like a world of words now made sense. They spoke to Mansa in a language she could understand, like a noisy room quietening down so that you could hear the conversation. As she worked, Mansa sounded out the letters, smiling to herself as she whispered the names written in white on the black t-shirts.

Anitha was the first name she had learned to write, even before her own. It was the name of her beautiful niece, although she had not seen her in nearly nine years. She also had a nephew, Prabukumar, who was born just after she left the village. She longed to meet him, but more than anything else she wanted to hold Anitha in her arms again. Every day she thought of her and, now that Mansa could write, she was able to scribble a few words asking how she was and what she was doing, but she had never heard back. Even if Anitha couldn't read them though, she wanted her to know that she cared, so she wrote every week, hoping someone could read them for her, living in the small hope that one day she would hear something back.

Mansa looked down at the ladies below working on the sewing machines, the needles pounding away as rhythmically as a train while they fed cloth to the hungry machines. Even over the noise she could hear Joshna chatting away, passing on the latest gossip. Joshna looked up and saw her smiling.

"Hey, what's the matter Mansa, you got nothing to do? You come down here and I'll give you plenty of work!" she said cackling through her broken teeth.

"I need more T-shirts, you're working too slowly! I'm going to be here until midnight waiting on you finishing!" Mansa replied smiling.

"Yeah, yeah!" she shouted, waving Mansa away with her hand as she turned back to her story. At that moment Jasmine arrived with a pile of black t-shirts stacked up in her arms, her hair pulled back in pigtails to expose her chubby young face. She had been brought to the factory a few weeks ago from a nearby village, so Mansa had taken it upon herself to show her the ropes and help her settle in. Due to the age difference she insisted on calling her 'Mansa Auntie' out of respect. Mansa was only thirty but she felt far older after all she had been through.

"Anna Ma'am wants to see you Mansa Auntie. Something important she says. She said to go right away. Anna Ma'am looked sad." Mansa's heart sank. She had only been called to the office on a few occasions. The most recent visit was to move her from the sewing machines up to the T-shirt printing station, but she knew that was as far as a woman like her could hope to go. She had loved learning her letters and the feeling of power it gave her, but she had been slow at it; the younger girls seemed to pick it up much quicker and their writing was far more beautiful. Their fingers were more nimble too and they could work more quickly. There could be no new job for her, she must be in trouble. Maybe it was because she talked too much. She did laugh a lot with Joshna and with Jasmine too. She could learn to be quiet though if she was given another chance.

In her old life nobody would want her now either. She would have been left by the roadside with nothing but a begging bowl and scornful looks. Maybe Anna Ma'am wanted her to leave too to get in some younger workers. People always wanted the younger ones. She had hoped here it would be different.

She walked slowly towards the brightly decorated office, her head hung low. The factory had become her home over these nine years, the women here her true sisters. This was the first time since she was a child that she felt part of something, like she actually belonged. There was nothing for her anywhere else, just the old way of life she had fought so hard to escape. Surely Anna Ma'am understood that. She couldn't be so cruel. Anna Ma'am had always been kind. Maybe she could ask to stay on and go back to the sewing machines or just sweeping the floor. There was always work to be done and she was happy wherever it was.

She took a deep breath outside the door, and then knocked timidly. Anna Ma'am came to the door, greeting her cheerfully, and led her inside, closing the door behind them. She beckoned Mansa to sit, perching on the edge of her desk as she faced her. Anna Ma'am's face was open and honest, smooth except for a pair of crow's feet at the corner of her green eyes. Her auburn hair was now streaked with grey and was tied in a bun behind her head, a pencil holding it firmly in position. Although originally from Belgium, she had been in Andhra Pradesh for over twenty years and almost spoke Telugu like a local, despite the occasional mispronunciation causing the ladies in the factory to chuckle.

"Mansa, thanks for coming. I hope you are well?" She looked at Mansa who nervously wobbled her head. "Tell me, how long have you been with us here at Fair Made?" Anna Ma'am asked, hands folded in her lap.

"Nine years in two days' time on June 13," Mansa replied without having to pause to calculate. She had counted every day here as a new life, celebrating the date of her arrival at the factory in place of her birthday each year. Anna Ma'am nodded slowly, her fingertips pushed together to form an arch, lips pursed tightly together. She spoke slowly, weighing the heaviness of each word carefully, as if stacking objects she feared would fall if she was too hasty.

"Mansa, what I am about to ask of you, I don't ask lightly. I know that this is your home, and that you have become a real part of our family. We love having you with us. However, I'm afraid I'm going to have to ask you to leave us for a short while."

The words hurt more than any punch or slap ever could. Her fears had been confirmed. She was no longer wanted. Mansa bowed her head fighting back the sting of hot tears. Her heartbeat pounded in her ears. Where could she go? This was all she had.

"Don't worry," Anna Ma'am said quickly, trying to allay her fears. "It is not forever, just for a few weeks at the very most." Mansa looked back up, lines of confusion creasing her face. Anna Ma'am continued her explanation. "You know that every year we send a number of women from here to different villages to educate the girls there, giving them the chance to come and join us here instead. That's how many found out about us, yourself included. If we hadn't gone to Jasmine's village recently, well, she would still be stuck there. Only by leaving here can we bring others back. Mansa, there is no easy way to say it but I am going to need you to go back to your old village Agnipatnam for a few weeks to speak on our behalf." Anna Ma'am paused for a moment as Mansa stared at her wide eyed, unable to respond from the shock. Anna Ma'am leaned forward.

"I wouldn't normally ask, but things there at the moment seem to be getting darker and darker. The Shalishi Sabha are meeting tomorrow to discuss what is to become of the poor girl who apparently 'seduced' the boy from the next village. Who knows what will happen, but if it goes as I fear," she paused and sighed. "Well, there's going to be a lot of trouble. Agnipatnam is like a firework at the moment waiting to explode. Added on top of that, it's Jatara season soon too. They will begin in a few days and there's talk that they are spending a lot on them this year. Apparently Chief Minister Kalluri has some big announcement to make, and whatever it is there is likely to be a backlash from somebody. I can only see life becoming more difficult there in the next few months. We need someone to go before this Jatara to speak to the girls who are about to be given to the temple, to offer them another way, a *better* way. Things are so bad that this is the perfect time to show them there is a life of freedom away from the pain they will suffer. With talk of Telangana in the air, this could be a time of change when they will actually listen and come to us."

"But, Anna Ma'am, me? I have never... how can I go back? In Jatara season? Surely, there must be someone else..." Mansa began.

Anna Ma'am gently took Mansa's hands in her own. "I know you are scared, but I see a strength in you Mansa. You are not the girl who came here nine years ago. You are a brave woman now. Also, no-one knows Agnipatnam like you do. You know the girls and their families. They will listen to you. I understand this will be painful, but if you are able to convince just one girl to come back here with you and save her from that evil, surely it will all be worth it? Think of the difference it has made to your life. It's in these dangerous times when we are needed most to bring light into the darkness."

Mansa opened her mouth then closed it before gently nodding her assent. She knew they were dark times indeed, especially with Jatara season almost upon them.

She closed her eyes and quietly mouthed a prayer for the strength to face her demons.

Chapter 3

Anitha

Anitha placed a hand on her little brother's clammy forehead. The fever had nearly burned itself out. Maybe this time he would be better. She pushed the strands of damp hair from his face and kissed him lightly on the cheek before looking around to check that her mother was still busy in the kitchen.

She knew that she should stay home and help, but it was impossible to be here while this was going on. She could think of nothing but her friend Javali and what would happen to her. All morning the men of the village had been walking past her hut on the way to the Shalishi Sabha, discussing what punishment they thought would be given. Some felt she would be cleared and left to go back home. Others thought she would have to pay a fine to the boy's family. Mr Harim said he thought they were likely to hang her as a lesson and Mr Charmar said he thought they would both be hanged. Anitha gasped so loudly when she overheard their conversation that it caused Mr Charmar to turn, spotting her crouched in the dust next to her hut. "I hope this teaches you not to be running around with higher-caste boys. Best you stay at home and help your mother," he said as he pointed at her accusingly with his beedi cigarette. With that they had turned and continued their walk towards the crowd which was swelling to the south of the village, all hoping to be the first to hear what was going on.

The Shalishi Sabha was meeting just outside the village.

From what she had heard the officials had all gathered in the late morning, some on foot, the others from further away in their big, black cars. Apparently one of the politicians had arrived in a car twice as long as everyone else's with windows so dark you couldn't see through them. She hoped to get a look at it and see, but Mother would never allow it.

Yesterday Anitha had pleaded to go, but it was no good. Her mother had scolded her. It was bad enough she had been friends with that girl, there was no need to remind people. She had to think of her reputation and that of her family. Besides, it was too dangerous to go anywhere near it. There was likely to be trouble too. Everyone always seemed to be angry at the moment and she had heard shouts from fighting most nights that woke her from her sleep.

Javali had been her best friend, apart from her own brother Prabu. Anitha went most days to get some milk from Javali's father's buffalo, and when her father wasn't watching, Javali would hand her a stick of sugar cane or a few of the sweets she had taken from his shop. Sometimes, if no-one else was home they would sit and talk or play with an old, creased set of cards that Javali had. It had taken   Anitha a while to learn the games, but now she knew all the cards and loved to play Rummy the most. She had even won a few times, although Javali would get annoyed when she did.

A few weeks ago when they had been playing, Javali had suddenly put the cards down and asked if she wanted to go for a walk to the river. They often played there if Anitha didn't have to help at home. As they wandered, Javali stopped by the mango orchard which had a small, dust path leading into it. When it was the right time of the year they would come here and sit on the ground eating mango after mango and laughing as the juice ran down their chins. They would get into trouble if anyone saw them, and she had been beaten on a few occasions when they were caught, but it was worth it because they were her favourite.

They walked past the track then Javali stopped and looked around, ducking under a bush and crawling through into the orchard before beckoning for Anitha to follow. Puzzled, Anitha obeyed. When they got among the trees, Javali took her by both hands.

"I have a secret I want to tell you, but you have to promise not to tell anyone else. Do you promise?" Anitha slowly wobbled her head in agreement, scared at what it might be. Her mother always knew if there was something which she wasn't saying. Javali looked about nervously.

"I was here last week picking mangoes. I was filling my scarf with them when I looked over there and saw..." she paused for effect, her eyes wide, "...a *boy*." She began blushing. "He came over and offered to help me collect the mangoes and then," she put her hands to her face and dropped her voice to a whisper, "he told me I was beautiful!" Anitha stood with her mouth wide open. "I had never seen him before, but he told me he was from Venapalli village. He said his family was very important because he was from the Reddy caste and he lived in one of the big houses and that he had his own motor bike, and he was so handsome! I told him that I had to go in case anyone saw me talking to him and he said that he had to see me again otherwise he would *die!*" She pressed her hands to her chest and sighed deeply.

"But you can't see him again. What would your father say?" whispered Anitha fearfully.

"Who cares? I have to see him again. He promised to take me for a ride on his motorbike! He was so handsome and kind and lovely! He looked just like Ranbir Kapoor from all the films and he liked *me*!" They heard a stick snap and turned to see a boy in short-sleeve white shirt sauntering towards them through the orchard. His hair was swept to one side and he had a wiry moustache that he rubbed his thumb and index finger over as if to flatten it. As he approached he raised his hand in greeting, the other tucked into his jeans pocket. Javali gasped and grabbed Anitha tightly by the shoulders. "That's him! He's come back!"

On seeing him Anitha instinctively turned and ran, terrified what would happen if her mother knew she was there talking with a boy. Not just a boy, but a higher-caste boy from Venapalli. Javali called after Anitha, but she ignored her, scrambling out from the orchard and running all the way home, not stopping once to look back.

That was the last time she had seen Javali.

Last night in her dreams she had heard Javali calling out to her, asking her for help, but as she tried to get to her the trees in the orchard had come to life, their branches reaching out and pulling Javali away while she screamed in terror. There was nothing Anitha could do as her friend writhed and kicked, unable to free herself as Anitha was left alone among the mangoes.

In her hut Anitha could hear shouting from where the crowd had gathered. She looked back a final time to check her mother was still outside, and then slipped into the crowd striding towards where the court was meeting. If she could just get there quickly and see what was happening then she could get back before her mother even knew she had left. She had to know that Javali would be alright.

She manoeuvred through those walking until she reached the circle which had formed around the council, everyone jostling for position to hear what was said. Many were shaking their heads and one or two were beginning to shout out. She pushed her way through until she was able to see. Six older men squatted on the ground, while Javali sat in the dust, her face streaked with tears. Her pink salwar kameez was torn and she hugged herself around her waist.

A younger man in a black jacket was standing and shouting out at the crowd, waving his hands in the air as he spoke. He had been interrupted from the back, and was raising his voice in fury as he strutted around like one of the cockerels that ran outside Anitha's hut. He was getting angrier and angrier as the crowd began to shout out. Rolling up a sleeve of his jacket and pointing straight at Javali he screamed out "She must be destroyed! Under the authority of Chief Minister Kalluri I sentence her to death by hanging!"

Within a heartbeat the place exploded. Anitha could feel the crowd behind her pushing to get forward, cries of protest ringing in the air as higher-caste men blocked their path, pushing them backwards. Fists were waved and the man next to her crumbled as a rock caught him square in the temple.

She fought to keep her feet as she was pushed, first one way and then another. Swept forward, the crowd parted, causing her to sprawl on the ground with hands outstretched, taking the skin from her palms. She yelped in pain, but quickly scrambled to her feet as legs pressed in around her. Through the crowd ahead of her she could see Javali being dragged away, thrashing her limbs as she screamed out. Helplessly Anitha reached out a bloodied hand, but there was nothing she could do.

Chapter 4

Mansa

Mansa arrived in Agnipatnam by late morning, the midday sun beating down on her as she walked the last three miles along the winding track to the village. Not a single rickshaw was going there today. The few she asked had shaken their heads and looked at her like she was crazy.

The belongings she carried on her head weighed down heavily, every step causing her to stoop lower under the burden. She wanted nothing more than to lie down and rest, but as she drew closer it became evident the Shalishi Sabha was already in session, and reluctantly she found herself swept along in the crowd of villagers heading to hear what was happening. The air was full of anxious conversations, neighbours talking in hushed voices as they discussed what they thought the judgement would be. Everyone had an opinion, and they all clamoured to make sure their thoughts were heard. Apart from during the Jatara, it was the most animated Mansa had ever seen the usually sleepy village of Agnipatnam.

Amid all the commotion, Mansa had entered the village without recognition. She covered her face with her scarf, hoping to avoid the looks of disgrace she feared she would encounter. She knew on any other day her return would set the idle tongues wagging and was glad to have been spared that much at least. Gossip was the favourite past-time here, the more slanderous the better.

Despite all this, she knew Anna Ma'am was right to send her, but it still didn't make it easy. It was nine years since she had left and she had not had the courage to return in all that time. She had longed to see her niece though, and the thought of being reunited with her was what drove Mansa on now.

When she arrived at the circle of bystanders watching the events, she noticed a few of the older ladies poking each other and turning to look at her, not even attempting to disguise their animosity. A few shook their heads and looked away while one spat on the ground near her feet. Mansa felt the old anger rising in the pit of her stomach, but managed to take a breath and counted to ten to remain calm. That was what Anna Ma'am had taught her to do. 'Don't react, take some time to let your brain engage before you do anything.' Many of the men near her now could have done with the same advice. While no more than an angry murmur ran through the crowd at the moment, there was a growing unrest as the speaker told of the measures he had taken in closing local brick factories. He described it as punishment for this insult which the village had allowed. He claimed that the actions of the girl were the responsibility of not just herself, but her family and the whole community.

Many of the men from the village held their plastic bottles of alcohol in clenched fists as they shot angry looks at the speaker. The members of the court squatted on the ground, the young girl in the centre of them quietly sobbing. Her top had been ripped down the front and she hugged herself to try and cover her nakedness from the hundreds of watchful eyes.

Strategically placed at the front of the crowd were a large

number of men who arrived with the speaker, the size of the group giving a subtle warning to any dissenters. They all nodded their approval to what was said, while a few Dalits from Agnipatnam turned and began to walk away in disgust, not bothering to wait for the verdict they suspected was coming.

"So today we are able to deliver justice and keep our great nation free from contamination. It is a responsibility we have, to keep our youth clean and pure, free from the evils that would gladly claim them," he continued, pounding his fist in his hand as he spoke, his demeanour like that of a fervent preacher. He walked from side to side making sure his message was heard and heeded by all present.

Mansa could clearly see the girl wiping her eyes with a dirty sleeve, but as she looked around there was no sign at all of the boy she had supposedly seduced. She watched the girl for a moment, her young face streaked with mud and tears. She had large brown eyes which Mansa could see were full of terror as she silently shook. No-one stood by to comfort her. The only person who looked at her was an old man with a bamboo stick, ready to strike her if she dared call out or move.

"She has committed a foul crime, which for centuries our ancestors have had to fight to stop. It is an immoral act which must be punished!" The men at the front nodded their silent agreement, faces solemn to show the gravity they felt the situation held. The Dalit men drank from their bottles, seething. Mansa looked again at the helpless girl being paraded without dignity.

"She is a corrupting influence, dirtying our society!"

Mansa could feel the old anger welling up inside her and before she knew it she had called out, breaking the flow of the speaker. "Where is the boy? Why is she the only one to be punished? This is not right!" Heads turned in her direction and many tutted as they recognised her. The speaker squinted in the sun, his face full of annoyance until a cruel smile upon his lips showed his recognition of her. He had often *visited* her during her days in Agnipatnam.

"Ah yes, and *you* are the one to tell us about moral rights and wrongs are you? Shall we all listen to your words on purity *Balamma*?" This drew a few chuckles from the front of the crowd as faces turned to sneer at her.

The use of her old name, Balamma, caused the heat to rise to her cheeks. She had not been called it in nine years, but in an instant it had the power to shackle her with the old insecurities she had once felt. She knew that despite all she had now become, here she would always be Balamma, never free from the stigma of whom she had been and what she had done. The village has a long memory; it never forgives or forgets.

Grinding her teeth together, she fought the urge to cower and condemn herself as worthless. These shackles *had* to be broken. Taking a deep breath she shouted out the words Anna Ma'am had made her repeat when she first left the village for the factory, "Balamma is no more. I am Mansa now," she declared proudly, her voice quivering slightly as she pulled back her shoulders, trying to stand tall.

Unimpressed, the speaker shook his head and turned his gaze away from her, not wanting to waste his time arguing with a Jogini when he had an important task to complete. He resumed his lecture to the crowd on the morality they were here to enforce. However, feeling empowered by her outburst, Mansa refused to be silenced.

"This isn't right!" she shouted again, wishing she had better words for such an occasion. "She's just a girl!" The smile disappeared from the speaker's face, his little patience with her quickly gone. He nodded to his left and she saw a large man begin to push back through the crowd towards her. She knew that she should move, she had to get away from there, but something rooted her to the ground. The girl's eyes were locked on her with innocent expectation, her mouth hanging open. No-one else had said a word in her defence and she doubted anyone would. Cursing herself, Mansa began to push forward through the crowd trying to reach the girl, the bag on her head knocking people aside as she edged her way forward.

"This isn't right!" she shouted again, people complaining as she barged them out the way while she blindly called out. A few people began to take up her shout though, nodding in agreement as she passed them.

The speaker's agitation showed as he grew louder, trying to reassert his authority on the restless crowd. His gestures grew wilder as Mansa pushed forward, continuing to cry out on the girl's behalf. The throng began to part for her, some now waving fists and jeering at the speaker. She continued forward, spurred on by the thought that if she could stir the angry crowd then just maybe she could help the girl. The politicians would have to listen if the crowd could make a loud enough noise.

The speaker's voice rose to a scream to cut through the disorder. The weight of his words caused the pushing and shouting to stop for a moment as he pointed at the girl and declared: "Under the authority of Chief Minster Kalluri I sentence her to hanging!" Mansa stopped, horrified, the bag slipping from her head as she screamed for them to stop. Hands gesturing wildly in the air, she yelled out, cursing the men for their cruelty.

Suddenly, Mansa felt a sharp pain in the back of her head, and then the world went black.

Chapter 5

Rupa

It was too late. Rupa knew that before they even arrived.

As the green and red van bounded away from the mud huts of the Dalit wada and up the hill to the Shalishi Sabha, they could see that all discussion was now well over. Anything which might have resembled an organised process was long gone; carnage now ensued. In front of them there was a crowd in total mayhem. Rocks were being slung while people were pushed forwards then backwards like the ocean in a terrific storm.

In his haste Stuart didn't see a woman was kneeling in the dirt to their left, wringing her hands and screaming, and narrowly avoided her with the van. Slowing, he edged cautiously forward, cutting through a group of men shaking sticks in the air as they rushed forward to join the crowd.

"Closer, we need to be closer," Rupa muttered as she shook her head. "Stuart, we need to get forward. Keep going!" Horn blaring, Stuart pressed on, weaving his way through the crowd, but it wasn't long before they were forced to halt by a large group in front of them waving their arms. Within seconds the van was swarmed. At every window a face peered in; some angry, others merely curious. Sweaty palms were pressed against the windows and Rupa could feel the sway of the bodies rocking the van as they were forced to a standstill. She leaned over from the back seat, nudging Stuart aside as she angrily pressed on the horn and gesticulated for people to move. However, the appeal was futile.

They were too tightly surrounded to see what was happening nearer the front of the crowd, but it was impossible to edge the van further forward in the mass of bodies. Trying to use the camera from here would result in seeing the press of the crowd and nothing more. Any footage would be worthless.

Stuart and Ben looked at Rupa for direction and she motioned upwards with her eyes. "The roof. Go!"

They grabbed their equipment and managed to force their way out of the van windows, then scrambled to the roof, hands grabbing and clawing at them as they climbed. Stuart fell backwards as someone tugged at his shirt, but Ben was able to reach out a hand and grab him, pulling him and the sound boom to the relative safety of the van roof.

"Stop trying to crowd surf and get your ass up here," Ben chided, a tight smile on his lips. Stuart gained his balance and nodded his thanks in return.

Ben turned his cap around, steadied himself on the swaying surface like a surfer meeting a wave, then slung the camera up to his shoulder and started filming. Now that he was here he didn't want to miss a moment of the mayhem. Things had been so mundane trekking from village to village carrying out interviews he was pleased to eventually have some action to film. The crowd seemed to stretch on forever as he searched through the lens for the cause of the commotion, scuffles breaking out everywhere.

"There, *there!*" Rupa practically screamed at Ben, spinning him by the shoulder and pointing about a quarter of a mile away to a small group gathered by a tree. As he brought the camera into focus he saw what Rupa was shouting about. A young girl of no more than thirteen was being held by two men as she whipped her head around frantically, a noose hanging loosely around her neck. He zoomed in managing to catch the wild look in her eyes as her impassioned pleas were met by stony faces. Like a crazed horse she bucked to get free, but it was to no avail; they held her too tightly.

"Damn it, we need to be closer! We should have been here sooner. Why isn't the crowd stopping them? We have to *do* something!" Rupa said exasperated as she ran her hands through her hair. The desperation welled up inside her as she helplessly watched the men gripping the trembling girl. "If they just knew that we were here, it might be enough to make them stop." There was no way forward in the van though, and who knew what would happen to them and the equipment if they tried to march through the crowd? She was so close, yet there seemed nothing she could do to stop the tragedy unfolding in front of them.

Rupa had been presenting for seven years. In that time she had come as close as she felt she could to compartmentalising her life, managing to see it as work she was able to walk away from it when she got home and shook the dust of Somalia, Romania or Mexico from her boots and poured herself a large glass of red wine. She was now able to content herself with what she was able to do, shining a light on injustice, rather than driving herself mad with what she couldn't do. "You are there to film the story, not be part of it." The sage advice of Rich, her mentor and friend echoed in her head now. Advice which had saved her career and sanity on many occasions.

Her first job at the Corporation had almost been her last after growing too attached to a family she'd interviewed in Mali. She had struggled to let go, with the overwhelming sense of frustration giving rise to depression. As a consequence she had spent the next year grounded in the UK until they felt she was ready to be back in the field. It had been a battle, but she was now able to create a wall to separate what was in her power to change and what was not.

Back here in India though, the walls she had spent seven hard years constructing had crumbled. It was far easier to be objective in a country with no connections, the translator and strange customs giving a sense of distance. But this was different. This was her motherland. She had been born right here in the state of Andhra Pradesh. She could relate to the stories that she had heard. Her baby sister Megana was only fourteen and headstrong. As she looked at this young girl struggling, she couldn't help but run through a series of 'what if's' in her mind. Rupa took a deep breath and tried to push them away. She wasn't to be part of the story, just to capture it. 'What if's' didn't matter, just reality.

She looked at the two men on the roof of the van with her and envied their degree of detachment. They were able to continue their filming without that connection. Ben had even sat there flippantly making jokes as they raced to reach here. It was just another job to them, their own immediate safety the biggest concern.

A big jolt caused them all to stumble slightly, but they managed to stay on their feet. Stuart glanced around nervously at the mob which now seemed to hold the van in its centre. Ben chewed gum, his face intense as he trained the camera on the tree. He was zooming in and out to cover the whole scene. About ten men were by the tree, most in trousers and faded shirts. They were animatedly discussing something as they nervously eyed the volatile crowd which had not yet reached them.

Suddenly a police siren sounded in the distance. Their lights could be seen flashing as they appeared from over the hill in a cloud of dust. As the cars approached, all eyes of the men by the tree turned to a well groomed man with slicked back silver hair in a black shirt and tie. Ben zoomed in to capture his expression. Almost imperceptibly he tilted his head, and two men hoisted the rope, jerking the girl straight from her feet and into the air like a rag doll. She swung from side to side, eyes bulging as she clawed at the noose tightening around her neck as her legs kicked frantically below her.

The camera shook slightly as Ben's hands trembled and he cursed under his breath. Stuart placed his hands on his head, letting the boom collapse onto the van roof.

"Megana! No! No! You can't. She's just a girl!" Rupa screamed as she ran over the bonnet and was swallowed into the crowd before Stuart was able to react and stop her.

A collective groan emanated from the crowd as they saw what was happening. The van shook as they charged forward like a stampede of wild animals.

The silver-haired man turned without even a look at the girl and was ushered into his waiting Mercedes, attended by three of his cronies. They pulled away as six police cars screeched to a halt by the tree. The police exited their cars as the girl swung in the air, trying to release herself from the noose that was choking the life from her. Without casting her a glance, they ran past and ploughed into the crowd, batons drawn while one officer fired a volley of shots into the air with his rifle.

Chapter 6

Anitha

Anitha ran all the way home, hoping that if she ran fast enough she could somehow leave the memory behind so that it would never catch up with her. Without a thought she dashed straight into their hut, oblivious to the tears streaming down her face and the bloody hand prints she had left on her yellow salwar kameez. She needed somewhere safe, to be away from the cruel world she had just witnessed. She wanted to be held in the comforting arms of her brother, but instead as she entered she was grabbed by the shoulders and spun around by her mother. She looked Anitha up and down, horrified by what she saw as Anitha gulped in air, trying to catch her breath. Before a word was spoken, her mother slapped her hard across the face.

"I do not even need to ask where you have been. Look at you! How could you after I told you not to go?" she demanded, waving a finger inches from Anitha's face. Anitha opened her mouth to try and explain all she had seen, but her mother only raised her hand. "I do not want to hear it, you wicked child. Tomorrow is your special day and you are off running around after this no good little *whore*, letting the whole village see your tears for her. Look at your clothes, the state of your hands," she said as she grabbed Anitha by the wrists and pulled her bleeding palms forward for inspection.

"But, but, the whole village was there. Javali was..." Anitha began choking out, the memory seared across her eyelids.

"I don't care who was there! The whole of Agnipatnam could have been but that wouldn't change anything. You are not the same as everyone else. You know that. You are different from that girl. To the rest of the girls here. You are   chosen. Special," she said, her voice softening as she cupped Anitha's face in her palms. "You will look so beautiful   tomorrow, just like Yellamma herself. You will make me very proud. Now, go and wash your hands and face, I have something I must show you."

Her mother walked out of the door, bowing as she left to an image of the goddess Yellamma adorned with a small garland of flowers. Anitha collected the cracked water jug and crouched in the corner of the hut, gently washing her grazed palms, wincing as they stung. She gingerly plucked a few small stones from the cuts then set about washing the tear streaks from her face, wishing it was that easy to wash away the afternoon's memories. Sighing, she stood and walked shakily to where her brother lay, a damp cloth across his forehead. She lent in and kissed him on the cheek, feeling the heat which had left that morning had now returned even hotter.

"Oh Prabu, I wish you were better. There is so much I want to tell you." She looked over her shoulder to check her mother had not returned. "I went today. I had to see what would happen to Javali, and they were horrible to her. They said they would hurt her, then they, they carried her away." She began to sob. "There was nothing I could do. She reached out for me, but I couldn't even touch her hand. If only you had been there. You are so brave, but I was scared, so scared." She buried her head on his naked chest, his flesh clammy on her cheek. "They took her away and I couldn't stop them. You can't go too. I need you to stay. Please be OK." She left her head there for a minute, feeling his chest rattling as it gently rose and fell with his shallow breath.

After a moment, she heard her mother's footsteps and she looked up to see her holding something wrapped in brown paper draped over her right arm.

"Did you feel your brother's fever is back?" her mother asked sharply. Anitha nodded, holding his hand in both of hers. "That's what happens when you disobey and go running off when I tell you not to. He was getting better until then. He's worse now than before, not that you would care." Anitha dropped her eyes, too ashamed to respond. "What did I do to deserve such a disrespectful daughter? Caring more about silly girls in the village than her own family." She stared at Anitha reproachfully before suddenly brightening. "The priest came today though. He said that after your dedication Prabu will start getting better again. He also brought you a gift from someone very special," she motioned to the present on her arm. "This is for you to wear tomorrow. Come," she said, beckoning Anitha with her free hand. Anitha stood coyly. She had never received a present before, let alone from the priest. Taking it in both hands she unwrapped the paper, being careful not to crease it.

Inside was a beautiful green and red sari. She gasped and looked up at her mother to check there was not some mistake. Her mother smiled at her. "See, didn't I tell you how beautiful you would look? I told you that you are special, more precious than those other girls. He gave me these too." She reached inside her blouse and pulled out two silver anklets which she let dangle from between her fingers. They spun slowly around, the bells gently chiming. Anitha watched them, mesmerised as the sunlight danced off of the silver. "All these from someone very important," she said handing them to Anitha. "What blessings on our family! You must put them away now though, you can wear them all tomorrow for your special day."

Anitha nodded, clutching the anklets tightly in her hand. They were such beautiful gifts; she couldn't wait to wear them. Suddenly though her face creased with worry. "What will I have to do tomorrow? What if I do it wrong and they want to take the gifts back? What if I make a mistake and Prabu doesn't get better?" Her mother stared at her reproachfully for a moment, hand on her hip.

"Don't say these things. He must get better. As long as you obey what I tell you everything will be fine. You will bring good fortune to our family. Everything will be good for us now, you will see," her mother said, flippantly waving her hand and forcing a smile to her face. "There is nothing to fear," she said flatly, more to comfort herself than Anitha.

Chapter 7

Mansa and Rupa

The arrival of the police seemed to have the desired effect on most of the crowd. Anyone from the higher-castes were long gone back to their homes, fearful of what they saw unfolding before them. Dalits on the fringes backed off, dispersing home to their wada. They had seen enough for one day and were eager to avoid any more trouble with the authorities, especially with the Jatara starting tomorrow. Over the years many of them had seen the futility of standing up to challenge authority, wounded by the repercussions that followed.

However, for others the police presence had an intoxicating effect. Already frenzied as Javali struggled for her life before their eyes, the sight of friends and neighbours being struck with clubs and fists poured fuel on the fire of their rage. As a volley of rifle shots pumped into the air, a guttural snarl went up from around Rupa, the crowd like a caged beast, mistreated for so long, that had suddenly decided to bite back. There was no telling what it would do next. It seemed that the beast had no idea either, lurching from side to side as it vented its rage on anything in its path.

Now off the roof of the van, Rupa had completely lost sight of the girl and was swept up in the wave that was crashing and breaking against the rapidly-formed line of police. The adrenaline she had felt as she leapt from the van had now been replaced by blind panic as she was shoved in the back and struggled to fight against the irresistible pull of the human wave. Hands were all over her, some pushing, others pulling, many desperate to show their anger, while others fought just to keep on their feet. Fists were raised all around her, insults hurled at the police as they mercilessly beat family members and friends of those in the crowd with sticks and the butts of their rifles.

Rupa bobbed up for air, looking around to try and gain some sense of direction. Fighting the flow she managed to twist around, despite arms hurriedly trying to drag her with them. She cried out in pain as she was jabbed in the ribs by a stray elbow. Winded, she clutched her side, trying to draw breath. Head down, she pushed on, through the tangle of arms and legs, eventually stumbling on to the dusty ground as she emerged from the back of the mob.

She remained there on her hands and knees for a moment, gulping in air. Disorientated by the surge, she looked around trying to navigate her way back to the van. She was surprised to see that she had been sucked along for a good two hundred metres, the van now a small island with only a few villagers sat around it in the dust, the tide of people ebbing away from it.

The boys were still on the roof of the van, intently surveying the crowd like lifeguards scanning the coastline for a sign of life. As she began to make her way to them she saw Stuart grab Ben's arm and point at her. They dived down from the roof, running towards her with the camera and boom bouncing on their shoulders.

"Are you alright?" Stuart asked as he reached her, holding her gently by the shoulders to support her. Rupa nodded from amid her daze, shell-shocked as she looked beyond them to the human wave still breaking itself against the police, frightened what would have happened if she hadn't manage to break free.

"What the hell?" Ben shouted as he caught up, red faced and out of breath. She looked up at him, shocked by the fury in his voice. "What's wrong with you? You could have been killed! You could have got us killed! What were you doing out there?"

"I just thought if I could somehow get there... then..." Rupa began, the words failing her as she pointed aimlessly toward the police.

"Then what? Have you seen what's happening there?" he asked, waving a finger at the madness a few hundred metres away. Another round of shots being fired punctuated his point. "Would you have flashed your 'PRESS' badge and made it all better? Maybe told them we were filming and they had to stop otherwise they would be in trouble? What did you think was magically going to happen?" he asked, hands on his hips. Rupa shrugged her shoulders, unable to collect her thoughts enough to respond. "You can't just run off. There are rules we follow for a reason. What have you achieved by your little jaunt? You have got to stop this saviour-complex *bull!*"

"Ben, give her a break," Stuart said, feeling her body shaking beneath his hands. "Now's not the time."

"You were saying the same thing a second ago! She's losing it. Look at her. We can't work like this. We've got a job to do and she's sabotaging it."

"C'mon Ben, she's back and she's safe. That's what

matters right now. We're all OK," Stuart said quietly, putting a hand on Ben's shoulder to placate him.

"OK? I am far from OK!" he said slapping off Stuart's hand and pacing around. "I have just stood on top of a van in the middle of a human stampede and filmed a little girl as the life was choked out of her, making sure the focus was fine to get a good shot. I could see the fear in her eyes. I could make out every single tear as it ran down her face, and you think that I'm OK after that?" He turned to face Rupa. "You think that we all don't want to do something, *anything* to stop it? But we can't. It's screwed up, it's *really* screwed up. But running off and putting yourself and us in danger isn't going to achieve anything." He lifted his cap and ran his hands through his hair. "After driving like madmen to get here, seeing *that* and surviving these crowds it's all been for nothing. We've achieved absolutely nothing!" He put his hands on his head and exhaled deeply, scuffing his boots around in the dust as he warred with his emotions. After a few moments he looked up at them, his usually jovial eyes now carrying a weight of responsibility. His voice softened, the anger ebbed out of it, replaced by weariness. "It's tough, I know. But out here *this* is all we have," he said pointing to the three of them. "We've got to watch each other's backs. I need someone I can rely on, and I don't think I can with you. Right now, your head's all over the place and you're a liability. I don't trust you and I honestly don't know if I can keep working with you."

"Ben, chill. Let's take a moment and..." Stuart began, but Rupa cut him off.

"Ben's right. I am all over the place. Seeing the girl,

well…" Her eyes began to well up with tears but she blinked them back. "I know I shouldn't have done it. We are here to film the story, not be part of the story. I should know that better than anyone. But being here has got under my skin. I guess I was sick of feeling hopeless, of not being able to change anything," she bit her lip, pausing for a moment before looking back at Ben. "Look, I'm really sorry. It won't happen again, I give you my word." They stood silently for a moment, each lost in their own thoughts as cries continued to ring out from the crowd. After a long moment, Ben nodded his head in acceptance of the apology.

The three of them stood silently, arms crossed as they watched the violence unfold before them. In the distance they saw the dead body of the young girl hanging lifeless from the tree as someone began to climb the trunk to release her lifeless form. From here she was merely a shape in the distance, but every detail of her face was etched in vivid colour into Ben's memory. He clenched his teeth, wanting to look away but finding it impossible to do so.

Stuart cleared his throat as more blue lights flashed in the distance, racing to the mayhem. He watched them for a moment as they screeched to a halt, officers in their brown uniforms springing from the vehicles and darting forward into the mob.

"It doesn't all have to be for nothing," he said, breaking the silence. They looked at him, waiting to hear what he had to say. "Just because we didn't stop anything this time, it doesn't mean everything has been wasted. If people watching this feel anywhere near as angry as we do, that's got to be a good thing, right? We can use this to show what's going on." Rupa and Ben both nodded. "But I say we don't just report on what we see. People will watch and say that's awful, then go back to their dinner. If we are going to bring any change we need to go after the people responsible for making it happen. We've got to be able to expose them, show them for who they are, and give people a way to respond."

"Good plan Stuart, glad to see there's something going on under those golden locks," Ben said, trying to lighten the mood. He looked at Rupa. "He's right you know. If we want to do anything we need to go after the people in power," he said, becoming focused again. "Check this out," he said, holding up the camera and rewinding the video to the man with the silver hair. Ben zoomed in to show his face as he directed the noose to be tightened. "Look at this smug git. See the way everyone is waiting for his orders? He's obviously some kind of ringleader. If we can begin by exposing him, well, it's a start isn't it?"

Rupa nodded slowly as she studied the small screen when a groan from behind caused them to look around and see a woman struggling to her feet. She clutched the back of her head, blood seeping through her fingers, as matted hair covered her face.

"Bloody hell!" Ben shouted, jumping slightly at her appearance. It reminded him of numerous zombie films he had watched, her eyes unfocused as she looked ahead, limbs not fully functioning.

Pushing herself up, she clumsily made it into a crouch, then toppled back to the ground. Rupa watched her intently, her forehead creased with worry. Ben looking despairingly at Rupa as he knew what was coming next.

"We have to get her in the van," she stated. Ben sighed. "We're not a bloody ambulance you know. We've barely got enough equipment for ourselves." They all looked over as she tried to stand only to tumble once more. Ben shook his head. "Alright, alright, but if you go cutting off an arm and there are no bandages to tie it back on, don't come crying to me."

They helped the woman up and managed to get her into the back of their van, Rupa trying to soothe her with words of Telugu as they gently got her seated. For all his moaning, Ben took charge, rinsing out the cut with some sterile wash, before winding a bandage around her head. Stuart, winced just watching, but the lady just sat staring ahead, her face almost motionless as they cleaned the wound. For all the blood, the cut wasn't deep, but there was a decent amount of swelling and some rogue stones which had crept in. Once Ben had finished she bashfully nodded her thanks to him, holding up a hand to refuse the painkillers he offered.

"What's your name?" Rupa asked in Telugu, sitting opposite her on the stool they used to keep equipment off the floor.

"Mansa," she answered, not looking at Rupa but staring around the inside of the van, fascinated by the recording equipment. It was an absolute state, full of empty chocolate bar wrappers and cigarette packets they had slung on the floor while working. The table in the centre was covered in magazines and a few copies of The Hindu newspaper they had bought when they'd collected the van from Hyderabad. Despite all their gear there was still a reasonable amount of room, with seats that doubled up as beds on their longer expeditions. Most of the seating area was covered in translations of interviews with words underlined and followed by copious explanations scribbled in Rupa's curly script in the margins.

She waited for Mansa's gaze to return to her then held up four fingers, asking Mansa to count them as she checked for concussion. After repeating the assessment a few times with varied numbers of fingers, Rupa judged she was alright. Rupa bent over and pulled a tepid bottle of water from a pack under the chair, offering it to Mansa. Mansa declined, but then accepted it on the second offer. She broke the cap and put the bottle to her dry lips, quickly gulping its contents down without stopping. Rupa pulled another bottle from under the chair which Mansa gladly accepted, despite Ben's raised eyebrows. This time she drank more slowly, savouring the refreshment. She couldn't remember the last time she had drunk anything, maybe not since the morning. Anna Ma'am had given her a bottle which she had brought in her bag, but she had finished that before arriving in the village, the journey hot and long.

Suddenly Mansa's eyes sprung wide open and she looked about her in panic.

"My bag! Where is my bag?" she asked Rupa.

Rupa smiled and called to Stuart to hold up the bag they had found next to her. It was battered and covered in dust, but was the right one, Mansa nodding her head in confirmation as she sank back into the chair in relief. Stuart passed it over and she quickly looked inside, relieved that nothing was missing.

Rupa waited till she had finished her check, then leaned forward. "Can you tell us what happened to you?"

"That's a long story," she replied, smiling sadly.

"I'd love to hear it."

"Are you sure? It's a very sad story too."

Rupa nodded placing a hand on Mansa's. "Only if you feel well enough to tell it."

Mansa touched a hand to the back of her head. "You mean with this? It's nothing, not compared to what has been done to me before."

"Mansa," Rupa began tentatively, "would you mind if I film while you tell us the story?" Mansa's eyes shot across to the camera, her face terrified as if it was a dangerous creature lurking in the corner. She held up her hands in refusal.

"No cameras, please. What would I say?"

"Don't worry about that. You just tell us your story; forget the camera is even there. Just look at me and tell me what happened."

Mansa's eyes remained wide with fear. "I may get in trouble. If I tell what has happened, people will not be happy. Some of those people are very important. What if they are made angry?"

Rupa weighed her words carefully. She didn't want to coerce Mansa into anything she was uncomfortable with, but at the same time it was difficult to suppress her excitement at the possibility of an honest interview. "We will do our best to make sure nothing happens to you. We can change your name if you want, and blank your face. Your story may be able to stop the same things happening to others as happened to you."

Mansa sat thoughtfully for a moment, then a look of resolve crossed her face. "OK, please, bring your camera. This is something which needs to be told." Rupa gestured to Ben for the camera, and he and Stuart leapt to their feet, getting the equipment ready in the cramped space of the van.

"So Mansa, can you start by telling us what happened today?" Ben zoomed in to catch the expression on her face, the bandage covering one of her eyes, while the other burned like fire.

"Today I arrived back in the village after many years away. I had heard the story of the girl, and that she was to be *tried* for her behaviour with an upper-caste boy." She laughed bitterly. "There was no trial though. They knew the outcome before they even arrived today. It was just a pretence of justice, those in power doing what they want and the rest of us being expected to do exactly what they say. They treat us like animals. The same as its always been."

"Who do you mean by 'us'?"

"Dalits. The untouchables. The backwards castes. Whatever name you want to give us."

Rupa nodded. She was well aware of the caste system and the group known as Dalits, who were seen as so low they were outside of the whole system. She remembered her own mother stopping her playing with a group of children because they were Dalits when she was young.

"And what happened to *you* during the trial?" Mansa instinctively touched the back of her head. She sighed.

"I couldn't let it happen. Once I would have, but not now. I am no longer Balamma, I am now Mansa. I spoke out for the girl and the punishment it brought was this," she said pointing at her head. Rupa waited a moment, letting the words hang in the air.

"Do you know who did it?"

Mansa shrugged. "I know the sort of men who did it. The individual doesn't matter. It was one of the high-caste men ordered to make us fear and respect those in power. It's their way of showing us to do as they say."

"And what do you think will happen now, after all that occurred today?" Mansa looked past Ben and out of the windscreen behind him. The crowd was all but subdued now, the police cars full of those refusing to cooperate, and the floor littered with the injured who had fought to be heard. She sighed heavily.

"I am not a smart woman. I am not educated, but I know nothing good will come from all this. Especially not with the Jatara starting tomorrow."

"What's the Jatara?" Rupa asked, the word like an old memory she couldn't quite place.

"You have never been?" asked Mansa, confused.

Rupa shook her head. "My family left India when I was only young."

"Then you are one of the lucky ones. It begins tomorrow, around the Yellamma temple. That is why there are so many people coming to the village. They will come from all around for the celebration. Many are already here, that is why there were so many people at the Shalishi Sabha. There is nothing else to bring them here, only the Jatara. Agnipatnam holds one of the biggest celebrations in Andhra Pradesh. It is the most auspicious occasion of the year," she said mockingly.

"So what is the Jatara? What happens?" Rupa probed.

"Every year before the Jatara a number of young girls are chosen and they are dedicated to the temple, some as young as five or six. This ritual is called the First Pattam. After this, they know that they will take no husband when they are older, but become married to the temple, becoming part of the goddess Yellamma herself. In some places they are called Devadasi or *servants of god*. Here they are known as Joginis. By either name they have the same duties. They will bring many blessings to their family." She gritted her teeth. "Well, that's what the girls will be told. In reality, they become temple prostitutes. Property of every man in the village, but never to be taken as a wife. That new life will begin for many of them tomorrow, their purity given to a village elder or priest once they have their first bleed. This ritual is the second pattam, often called '*The Night of the Girl Virgin*'. Sometimes both pattams just happen on one night. Whichever man is chosen by the elders receives the *honour* of deflowering the girl. Sometimes, after the first night, they keep the girl for a few years, buying her gifts and jewellery. Normally though, they discard her quickly and then she is used by all in the village, first by the upper-castes, then down through everybody until she is also used by the Dalit men. She cannot say no. She must do it as service to the goddess."

"When you say she is *used* by the men in the village, I assume that means..." Rupa asked for clarification on the film.

"Sex work," Mansa stated. "After that first night their life will be a constant misery, cleaning the outside of the temple, but never allowed to worship there as they are still a Dalit and they will 'pollute' the holy place. Untouchables, so unclean they shouldn't touch the inside of the temple and make it dirty, and yet it is completely fine to use them for pleasure by joining bodies. As I said, I am only a simple woman, but surely that is not right?"

Rupa shook her head in disgust at what she had heard. "Do people not try to stop it?"

Mansa shook her head sadly. "It is now illegal, but that makes no difference. Laws exist here only to be broken. They are not worth the paper they are written on. Why would the police or priests stop it when they are the ones to benefit from it? They claim it is an honour to be a Jogini, but it is only a life of heartbreak and misery."

"How do you know so much about these Joginis?" Rupa asked.

"Because I was one."

Chapter 8

Anitha

Later that day, a lady called Renuka arrived at their hut. She was older than Anitha's mother by quite a few years but shorter than Anitha, even though Anitha was only eleven. Her grey hair was all bunched together and looked like it had not been washed for quite some time. It hung down past her waist in strands as thick as sticks of bamboo and swung about as she walked. Anitha had never seen hair quite like it, although she had seen the lady many times at the Yellamma temple, especially during the celebrations. Her mother had told her that this lady was very important as she was the chief Jogini; she had faithfully served the goddess Yellamma for many years. However, she was now older and new Joginis were needed to appease the goddess.

Before she had arrived, Anitha's mother had warned her to show complete respect. It was very auspicious for Renuka to visit their home so Anitha had to remain silent unless spoken to.

As Renuka entered, Anitha's mother bent low to the ground, touching her feet as a sign of reverence. She looked at Anitha and gestured with her eyes for Anitha to do the same. After, as Anitha stood, she stared at the lady's forehead which had three yellow stripes pasted on it, with a large red dot dabbed in the middle. Her eyes were like a small bird's and they constantly darted around from Anitha's face to her brother and then to Anitha's mother. She made Anitha nervous and she was relieved when her mother told her to go make the chai.

Standing in the corner of the hut, Anitha kept her back to them, sprinkling the tea leaves and spice into the pot while she listened intently to all that was being said. The two women sat next to each other on the floor, talking in hushed tones.

"I have come to make sure she is ready for tomorrow," Renuka said, placing a wooden bowl before her mother who reached inside her sari and pulled out a number of rupee coins. Renuka moved the bowl to her side and sucked her browned teeth that looked like kernels of burnt sweet corn. "It is a big honour to become a Jogini, I hope she realises how blessed she is?" As Renuka spoke, Anitha could feel eyes on her back.

"Oh yes," her mother stated, "it is a big honour. She is very excited."

"She is dark-skinned this one, but not too dark. I think she will be pleasing to Yellamma, as long as she listens to all that I tell her."

"She will listen and obey," her mother said, as a reassurance to Renuka and a threat to Anitha. They were quiet for a moment and Anitha brought over the small clay cups of chai and placed them in front of the ladies, her hands shaking slightly. She then stood, watching while they drank in silence, an occasional slurp the only sound.

Once she had finished, Renuka patted the dusty floor next to her, motioning for Anitha to sit. She took Anitha's chin in her hand and stared into her eyes. Anitha tried not to be afraid, but the woman terrified her. One of her eyes was green, the other brown, and the green one moved as she spoke.

"Let me tell you of Yellamma," she said, gesturing with her finger to the portable shrine of the goddess which she had removed from her head on arrival and left next to the door of the hut. Anitha had always been interested by the blue-faced Yellamma, finding it quite peaceful, but the silver face and bulging eyes on this one frightened her. It was almost as large as Renuka who had carried it and was decorated by peacock feathers and cowry shells. Garlands of red and yellow flowers adorned the goddess's neck and sari.

Lighting an incense stick, Renuka inhaled the smell of sandalwood, the fragrant smoke surrounding them and quickly filling the small hut. Anitha's mother shuffled in closer, eager to hear the story recounted. Renuka began, her voice low and husky as if letting them in on a secret.

"Yellamma was very beautiful indeed and she was married to a wise man named Jamadagni. Every morning she would walk to the river to collect water for her husband to use in worship. She would collect sand by the river, using her concentration to form it into a pot she could keep on her head. However, one day everything changed. When she got to the river there were two nymphs frolicking in the water. Rather than turn away she sat and watched them, filling her head with impure thoughts." Her green eye focused on   Anitha who slowly moved her head from side to side, though she did not understand what this meant. "When Yellamma tried to make a pot that day she couldn't concentrate and it crumbled, covering her in water," she said, mimicking the flow of the water over her head with her fingers. "Panicking, she tried again and again to make another pot," Renuka said, trying to mould the mud on the floor in front of her into the shape of a pot. "She couldn't though and she had to go back to her husband and explain what had happened. Straightaway he knew the impure thoughts she had felt causing her to lose the concentration she needed." Anitha and her mother sat transfixed by the story, waiting to hear what happened next, even though her mother had heard the story recounted many times.

"Her husband said nothing, but handed her a necklace. When she put it on suddenly her whole body became covered in red spots! She fled, roaming the mountains, begging for food and shelter, until one day she came across two gods who took her in and taught her how to cure all sorts of illness. She healed herself and returned to her husband, once more beautiful and full of youth, but she was not welcomed. Instead, he was furious! He ordered his sons to chop off her head," she said, slowly drawing her hand across her neck. Anitha gasped.

"The three eldest sons refused," she said, holding up three bony fingers. "In his anger their father cursed them to live as women." As she said this she folded the fingers back into her palm. "But his youngest son, Parasurama, carried out his father's wish. He found his mother hiding with an untouchable woman and beheaded them both. Jamadagni was so pleased with his son that he granted him one wish. And do you know what that wish was?" Anitha shook her head, mouth open as she listened intently. "He asked for his mother to be brought back to life!" Renuka said, cackling and clapping her hands together.

"But her husband in his confusion placed Yellamma's head on the untouchable woman's body and the woman's head on Yellamma's body! Therefore, Yellamma was forever part high-caste: part Untouchable." She stared at Anitha then pulled her chin up with her fingers, her long nails digging into Anitha's soft flesh. "Yellamma suffered greatly in this life. So also must we suffer." She held Anitha with a stare for a moment and then released her fingers from Anitha's face.

"W-w-what must I do?" Anitha stuttered. Anitha's mother shot Renuka a worried look, but Renuka leaned forward, her face only inches from Anitha's.

"There are many things you must know, little one. Many duties to fulfil. Do you know what they are?"

Anitha shook her head, her mouth too dry to speak.

Renuka leaned forward, being sure Anitha was taking in all she said.

"The most important is that you must never complain. Never! Even if you are hungry or in pain, a Jogini never complains. We accept what is difficult just as Yellamma did. Also, you will be the wife of no man. You will be married to the temple. Tomorrow you will be given your wedding band, the thaali necklace to show you belong to no man. This will be tied to represent you are given over to Yellamma only. What else? Ah yes, on Tuesdays and Fridays you must beg at five houses at least. You may be given rice, maybe cooked or uncooked. If you are very lucky a few rupees may be spared for you. This is how you will feed yourself." She held up her wooden begging bowl to illustrate the point. "You will have many visitors, and you must always do as the men ask. You must never turn them away." At this point she shot a knowing look at Anitha's mother who swallowed, but nodded.

Anitha sat quietly trying to remember the different duties she must complete. How would she manage to do all that had been said? She didn't even understand what half of them meant.

"Come," Renuka said, rising to her feet. Unsure, Anitha rose, watching her as she picked up her golden bell and rang it to ward off evil spirits. She waddled over to the Jagha shrine and pulled out a silver plate next to it which had several silver oil lamps on it. Lighting them and several sticks of incense, she began to chant a mantra as she encircled the shrine of the goddess. Wiping the shrine's head with a cloth, she reapplied the yellow haldi and placed a red dot of kumkum between her eyes. Anitha's mother brought over a few rice balls and a banana on a leaf and placed them before the shrine. After the ritual, Renuka took the yellow paste and wiped it on Anitha's forehead before feeding her a small part of the banana.

"You may now ask the goddess a question. If the answer is 'yes', she will allow me to lift the Jagha in the air. If it is 'no', then it will remain on the ground. Understand?"

Anitha nodded, too scared to speak. She stared at the statue for a long moment fearful of the response she would receive. Even though it was a statue, it felt to Anitha as if it was watching her every movement.

"Ask now!" Renuka snapped. "The goddess does not want to wait for you forever."

Anitha swallowed. There was only one thing she really wanted to know. "W-w-will m-my brother b-be made b-b-better?" she stuttered. Renuka closed her eyes and approached the Jagha, taking it firmly in both hands. As she gripped it

Anitha and her mother watched in silence, hearts thumping in their chests. Knees bent, Renuka stood for a moment, and then ever so slightly they saw the Jagha rise from the ground. They both let out a huge sigh of relief, and at that moment Prabu murmured in his sleep and they all turned to look at him. Anitha ran over and kissed him on the forehead, the fever feeling as if it had left him.

"The spirits will leave the boy, but only if you fulfil your duty to Yellamma. The goddess demands obedience." Anitha nodded her head furiously, determined to do everything she could to help. Renuka turned to Anitha's mother. "She will bring many blessings to this home. Your son will be fit and strong again. Soon he will be returned to you in full health."

"Thank you," her mother said, bowing her head, eyes brimming with tears. Renuka curtly nodded her head and Anitha's mother bent down and touched her feet once more.

Renuka walked over and stared Anitha in the face. "My time in the temple is over, but yours is soon to begin." Anitha trembled, feeling as if the lady was looking inside her, seeing her darkest terrors. "You must be brave. You are soon to be the goddess. The goddess shows no fear."

Chapter 9

Mansa

She had warned them. This place was not safe for outsiders, especially not during Jatara. She had told them her whole story leaving nothing out, but they hadn't listened. If they had they would have driven away, leaving this place far behind them. She had done all she could. It wasn't her concern what happened to them now. She had been sent here for a reason by Anna Ma'am and she didn't intend to let her down.

She had to hurry, by this time tomorrow the second pattam would be under way. Once the girls were deflowered there wasn't much she could do. They became the property of the temple, bound to it for life. At that point it would be nearly impossible for them to then leave their life as a Jogini. She intended to fight right up to that moment though. To save them from the life she had endured. If it hadn't been for Anna Ma'am she would still be there, trapped. Forced to pleasure countless men and eke out a living by begging in the streets.

It had not been easy for her to leave Agnipatnam. Her mother and grandmother and great grandmother had all been Joginis for as many generations back as she could remember. They wouldn't have understood her decision to turn her back on the temple, her family, the whole community. For them, that was everything. But they had not been given the choice she had. When Anna Ma'am arrived speaking of another way of living, it was the first time she had been able to *choose* something for herself. To take power over her life; her body.

She had lost so much, but every day in the factory she now counted as a blessing. It felt like life had begun for her from the moment she arrived there.

She was the only one that responded that day though. Her sisters in Yellamma were bound to the community and temple by their superstitions and fear, worried that if they turned their back on the temple, Yellamma would punish the whole village.

She had seen some of women earlier, bitterness in their eyes as they saw her return, her very presence antagonising to them. She knew droughts or bad fortune suffered had been laid at her feet for choosing to leave, people too immersed in the superstition to see that she had nothing to do with it. Luckily for Mansa though their venom was diluted with so many pilgrims around, the events of the day summoning everyone's attention.

The slow rhythm of daily life in the Dalit wada had been completely disrupted and the usual jobs were ignored as people checked on family members and nursed their wounds. She could feel the whole place simmering, bent but not broken by all that had happened. The normally quiet dusty streets were packed, no-one wanting to miss out on the latest gossip as they exchanged stories, guessing at what the coming weeks were going to hold. Arguments broke out between friends, some fearful of what else could happen to them, while others were enraged, ready to fight once more.

As Mansa walked the familiar dirt paths that wove in and out of the closely-packed huts she could feel eyes watching her as she passed, the noisy chatter silenced for a moment. Many knowing glances were exchanged and a few spat on the ground or turned their faces away.

She passed a group of ten or so men sprawled on the side of the road. Their eyes were glazed as they drank the clear liquid from their plastic bottles and smoked beedi cigarettes, the thick smell of the fumes filling the night air.

"Hey Balamma, I've been waiting for you for so many years! Why don't you come here and say hello?" a rickshaw driver named Gopal called after her in slurred tones. He had been a regular visitor, striking her on occasion when he was drunk.

Mansa bowed her head, not wanting to make eye contact. The pain throbbing behind her eyes felt as if her head were being used as a duppa drum for the Jatara. She tried to get past quickly, shame burning her cheeks until she began to remember the prayer they recited every morning in the factory. "You are unique. You are special. A child of God, not a slave." She repeated it over and over, until she felt its truth and began to pull her shoulders back and hold her head high. She had no-one to fear, nothing to be ashamed of. They were the ones who should feel shame for how they had treated her.

With that prayer in her head, she found strength to ignore the looks that had stung as she pushed on through the crowds towards the local chai shop. She knew that this was the best spot to hear the news about which girls were to be paraded and deflowered at the Jatara.

As expected it was heaving tonight. Her old neighbour Padma still ran it, shouting instructions at her two young daughters who were a year or two older than her niece. One stirred the cauldron of chai, throwing in more masala and sugar as directed by their mother. The other ran back and forwards, collecting 3 rupees for every clay cup she served.

It was impossible to get to Padma with it being so busy, so Mansa decided to join a group of ladies at the back who were squatting on the floor. As she approached, one of the ladies nodded at another and they closed in the circle, continuing to chat as if they had not seen her. Again, she repeated the prayer in her mind, trying to stop the rejection piercing her heart.

Around her were ladies she had spent the days with talking and passing the time. Ladies she had helped in childbirth. Ladies who had been beaten and come to her for   advice. She breathed deeply, trying to keep it all in. Then, almost imperceptibly, she saw one of the younger women in front of her shuffle round to make a space for her. She recognised the girl's face, but took a moment to remember her name. Anjali, she thought, memories slowly returning to her. Nine years was a long time and they had not spoken often due to the age difference. She would have only been about ten when Mansa had left the village but now she was nearly twenty. Mansa hesitated, unsure whether this was an invitation. The girl looked up at her and smiled.

"Come," Anjali said, patting the ground next to her. "You must be tired Auntie. It has been a long and difficult day for us all." Mansa nodded, too grateful to speak. She could feel the eyes of many of the women watching her as she slowly lowered herself, her battered body aching. The older woman with Anjali mumbled something then stood to leave. Anjali shrugged at her then turned to Mansa, speaking barely over a whisper. "My mother says I should not be speaking with you. That you bring trouble with you. Tell me Auntie, is that true?"

"It is not my desire to bring trouble," Mansa responded with a weary sigh, "but sometimes it seems to follow me around."

"There was a lot of trouble today Auntie. Is that where you hurt your head? Is it paining you?" she asked, a concerned look on her face.

"It's fine," Mansa lied. "Many people were hurt worse than me."

"Javali was hurt the worst of all," Anjali said sombrely. "Some of the high-caste men said she deserved what happened, but I don't think she did. My brother was hurt too. He was hit by the police, but he seems to be alright. He is at home now. It has been a terrible day. Tell me, did all this happen because you came back Auntie? Is that what Mother meant about bringing trouble?" Mansa felt a pang of guilt, and then reminded herself that when all this began she was far away, back safely at the factory. The superstition ran deep here though. It was stifling. Out in the city she felt free to be herself, able to think, but back here in the village it felt like the very air they breathed was full of lies and superstition which were inhaled by one person, then passed on to the next. It was difficult not to inhale the poison too.

"This had nothing to do with me, though some people will always try and blame it on me," Mansa said. Anjali nodded and sipped her chai thoughtfully.

"How is your sister? Puja isn't it?" Mansa asked. Anjali's

older sister had been dedicated not long before Mansa had left. She was a beautiful young girl, always full of mischief. She was one that Mansa had tried to persuade to join her in the factory but she had been too fearful of being rejected by her family.

Anjali moved her head noncommittally from side to side. "Puja left years ago for Mumbai. I have not seen her in many months. After her first night, she was very lucky. The man was a rich landowner from Venapalli. He was besotted with her and would buy her new saris and give her bracelets, some of them made of gold. He said he loved her and would ask her to visit him most nights, even though his wife would get angry and curse her. He was old and fat but Puja was quite happy. She only had one man to worry about."

"So what happened?" Mansa asked, sipping her chai, knowing the probable outcome.

"She got pregnant. She thought he might be happy if it was a boy, but once she told him he told her never to come to the house again. If he saw her after that he would walk past quickly and pretend he didn't know her. This made her very sad for a long time." Mansa knit her eyebrows together at the memory. "The gifts stopped too. Puja ran out of money and sold all the jewellery to survive. She was scared of how she would live with a baby on the way, so she decided to follow many of the girls from Agnipatnam and go to Mumbai to work in the brothel. She said if she had to please men that she may as well get paid for it."

"When did you last see her?" Mansa asked sadly.

"Last year at the Jatara." Anjali smiled wistfully. "Now

she has a girl and a boy, they are both beautiful. They will be as beautiful as her." She turned her attention back to Mansa. "Are you going to stay for the Jatara Auntie? Mother says this year will be the biggest there has been."

"Yes, I will be here. Tell me, were there many girls dedicated earlier this year?"

"Many Auntie. It seems Yellamma demanded a lot this year. Maybe with all this trouble not enough were dedicated." Mansa gritted her teeth together to keep from arguing, heat rising to her cheeks.

"And the second pattam. Will there be many girls given this year?"

Anjali thought carefully for a moment, slowly counting on her fingers as she mumbled to herself. "I think probably five. There is Anjamma, Shyamala, Shruthi, Chenamma and maybe one or two more I can't remember." Mansa nodded sourly. There was normally only about three here in Agnipatnam. Despite being outlawed, the practice still seemed to be thriving. The numbers gathered to celebrate were proof of that. Chief Minister Kalluri was very content to let it continue, encouraging others in the practice. No doubt it would be sure to grow if he was re-elected in the coming month. Something had to be done to stop him.

Some believed the creation of a new state might mean a new future for the Joginis. Mansa had serious doubts whether the new state of Telengana would make any difference to the lives of the Joginis here in Agnipatnam though. She suspected that no-one in power would care enough to actually stand up and do anything, especially if it might lose them votes. A lot of people would be angry if the rules to abolish the dedications were actually enforced.

Mansa sighed, overwhelmed by the task ahead of her. At least she knew who the girls and their families were. That gave her somewhere to begin. This was why Anna Ma'am had given her the task. She hoped that she could repay the faith that had been shown in her to make a change.

As she stood to leave, Anjali helped her to her feet and smiled.

"It is good to see you again. But be careful Auntie. Please don't get into any trouble." Mansa smiled sadly and nodded. I wish that was something I could promise, she thought.

Chapter 10

Rupa

The back of the battered news van was now a hive of activity. After finishing the interview with Mansa, Rupa had immediately told Ben to play it from the start and she translated for them. As she started to explain the Jogini system, Stuart shook his head, eyes narrowed in disbelief.

"Now this is a story which has to be told!" Ben said lighting a cigarette and waving it around excitedly. "So let me get this right, at this Yellawhatever place, these girls are married to the temple so when they hit puberty they can't take a husband, but they are then used by any of the blokes in the village who want them?" Rupa nodded, her face taut. Ben wiped the sweat from his brow. "That is something messed up right there."

"To begin with they are used by whoever the village elders decide to give the *honour* to. It could be a priest, one of the elders themselves or someone of influence in the community. After they no longer want them they are passed on to other high-caste men in the village, then the lower castes and eventually anyone who wants to use them. They have literally no say, they are not allowed to refuse any man who wants them."

"It's not exactly a big village though, I mean, surely gossip gets around. Would the wives not know this is going on and stop their husbands doing it? Surely they must have some idea?" Stuart asked.

"Well, that's the thing. Mansa said that sometimes the wives actually *encourage* their husbands to visit the Joginis because they believe that the girls *become* Yellamma, the goddess, and it is her they are with," Rupa said. "She says that a bit later on. They are seen as bringing luck to the family through the act."

Ben gave a disdainful laugh. "Some sick guy must have come up with that one. That is twisted."

"How can you tell that someone is a Jogini?" Stuart asked.

"You've already seen some in the crowd. They all had yellow stripes on their forehead with a red bindi dot in the middle of the stripes," Rupa replied.

"But there were loads of them!" Ben said.

"Apparently lots show up during this Jatara as it's the time for them to make money begging because it's an *auspicious* occasion so people are more inclined to give. There are lots of people here worshipping Yellamma, which means the Joginis have a high status during the festival."

"I bet there are a lot of horny men here too during the festival," Ben commented.

"Just thinking out loud, but I'm assuming that there isn't much in the way of contraception out here in the villages? Surely if just one of those guys has HIV then..." Stuart said, letting the thought hang in the air.

Rupa grimaced. She took a moment to compose herself and then a familiar look came across her face as she began to formulate a plan. "Right, Stuart, get researching the HIV/ AIDS rates here in Andhra Pradesh. Ben, see what you can find on the history of it all. Where did the practice develop, is it in all of India or just regional? I'm going to see what else I can find out about these Jataras."

They lapsed into silence as a frenzied few moments on their computers ensued, before they began calling out their findings.

"The dedications happen mostly in Karnataka, Andhra Pradesh and Maharashtra. Of all the Southern states in India, HIV in Andhra Pradesh is the worst with 500,000 cases, then Maharashtra with 420,000, then third is Karnataka with 250,000. Looks like there is a link there to me," Stuart called out.

"Devadasi women used to learn special dances; it was seen as a bit of an art form by the looks of it. They were held in high social status in the courts but then the British rule tried to change things and they ended up losing status over many years and basically becoming prostitutes. The practice of dedicating the girls was outlawed in the 1980s," Ben said. "So, it's now illegal, but looks like it is still going on. This site puts the figure near 250,000 girls involved!"

"This is massive," Rupa said leaning back, gazing up at the dented roof of the van with her hands folded behind her head. "This was my state. How was I oblivious to it all?" she muttered to herself. "Well, surely any filming we do *has* to focus around this? Are we all agreed?" They both nodded. "Right," she said, standing and grabbing a pen and a napkin leftover from an earlier restaurant trip in Hyderabad. She scrawled 'Jogini' in the middle of the paper and began writing notes around it. *Mansa interview - Jogini survivor. Yellamma temple - research?? Need interview with girl before dedication. Priest interview? Find out history. Who chooses girls? Facts and figures.* As she scribbled, one thought kept coming back to her mind.

"Ben, play the rest of that interview." They sat around the screen and she translated Mansa's words verbatim.

"But you must go now. This is not a safe place for you to stay. You are outsiders and this is a very dangerous time." "What makes it so dangerous?" "Chief Minister Kalluri and his partner Mr Chaudhury. They will not like you being here and making these sorts of films." "What can you tell me about these men?" "Kalluri is Chief Minister in Andhra Pradesh and Mr Chaudhury is the head of the high-caste party. Their two parties have joined together to rule. The elections are next month and they want to retain power, but there is a new party, the Dalit Freedom Party, who are close to taking over. There are many here from the lower-castes unhappy with all that is happening and they want to see the Dalits take power. However, Kalluri and Chaudhury will do anything to keep their control. They will see you as a threat to get rid of, showing up and making these films. Especially with all of the trouble recently with people fighting to create a new state. It is not a safe place for anyone, especially you. Please, you must leave now." On the screen Mansa leaned forward, anxious she was understood.

Rupa motioned for Ben to stop the tape. In capitals on the napkin she wrote; CHIEF MINISTER KALLURI and MR CHAUDHURY.

"Let's have a little look and see if these delightful gentlemen are anything to worry about shall we?" she said, tapping away at the keys on her laptop.

"Hey, this guy looks familiar," Ben said, double clicking to enlarge an image of Mr Chaudhury shaking hands with a voter. He snapped his fingers. "It's that guy, the one from the hanging!" He spun his screen around so that they could both view it too. Pointing at the image he said, "the silver-haired dude. Well, that explains a lot."

"Real friendly politician," Stuart said, shaking his head. "Bet you don't see him walking round kissing many babies." It didn't take much sifting through recent talks Mr Chaudhury had made on education and employment before a recurring theme became apparent.

"'Chaudhury and Kalluri bribe voters to gain state,'" Ben called out.

"'Dalits silenced in Andhra to give Kalluri/Chaudhury victory,'" Stuart added.

"'Bully tactics secure Andhra stronghold,'" Rupa chipped in. She began to skim-read the article, pausing about midway through. "'The 2009 elections in Andhra Pradesh looked all but lost to MP Giri Kalluri of BTN until his party jumped into bed with the BSP to help them regain power. A moderate party till then, the BTN BSP coalition has now become synonymous with violence and intimidation in Andhra Pradesh. It has created a chokehold of fear over the state that it doesn't want to loosen. Rumours abound of preventing Dalit voters entering stations in certain strongholds, narrowing the chances of the ever growing Dalit Freedom Party. Their promises to rid the police force of corruption have become farcical, with Kalluri's role now seeming to stretch from Chief Minister to Chief of Police too.'" Rupa paused, looking up from her screen. "There are some pretty harsh words in here. Keep looking guys. And make sure you check out the reporters. We don't want to go into this following some extremist with a vendetta against them. Make sure the sources check out." She scanned numerous articles, all seeming to tell the same story of intimidation and pressure, although there was little actual evidence presented.

There was a spate of stories in 2012 about the coercion, although there was nothing about the current campaign or responses to the idea of a new state. All recent press seemed to be largely positive, mostly referencing the Dalit Freedom Party as the perpetrators of violence and disorder which Kalluri and Chaudhury were needed to control. The two men were portrayed by some as almost demigods, holding the state together and leading it from the darkness to the light, fighting to bring peace and justice for all.

In such a polarised country Rupa was not surprised by the different views, but it was perplexing that at such an important stage in the elections Chaudhury's fiercest critics had nothing to say against him. She pulled up the three most prominent reporters speaking up against him; Sagar Raj, Rambabu Krishna and Sai Kumar. She gave each of the boys one to research.

She chose to look at Sagar, discovering he studied Journalism at Delhi University. After graduating he began writing for *The Hindu* newspaper and spoke out on human rights issues. He was tragically killed in a car crash in June 2012. Next to it was a photo of the over-turned car, numerous stern-faced police officers standing around the scene in their starched brown uniforms. Her heart skipped a beat and she jumped as she looked round to find Ben hovering over her shoulder. "I checked out this guy, Rambabu Krishna who was pretty mouthy. He was from Mumbai, began in a few local papers writing sports stuff then moved into critiquing politics. He was from a rich family but from the comments he seemed a bit of a revolutionary, kicking off about lots of social issues. He was a bit of an artist too by the looks of it. Drew some satirical cartoons, some of our old friends Kalluri and Chaudhury. They're actually pretty funny. Look, there's one here of them like an old married couple. It's got Kalluri just agreeing to everything Chaudhury says to him," he said holding up the screen for Rupa to see. She raised her eyebrows, waiting for him to get to the point.

"So anyway, seems like this Rambabu guy was behind a bit of a campaign aiming to bring down Chaudhury and Kalluri. Funny thing is, in the build up to this election he was found dead in his apartment, although police reports claim there was 'nothing sinister'," he quoted, using his fingers to draw speech marks around the last two words.

At that moment, Stuart's head popped up. "First article here, 'Sai Kumar was tragically hit by a speeding car in 2012 and died in hospital due to his injuries. The driver was never found.'" They looked at each other, wide-eyed.

Ben was the first to speak.

"I'd say we might have something to worry about."

Chapter 11

Mansa

She had managed to visit three of the dedicated girl's houses, but for all the good it did she might as well have just stayed at the factory. The families looked at her like she was the enemy, trying to steal their daughters away from them. No matter what Mansa said, they wouldn't listen, some shouting and swearing, driving her from their homes.

The last home she came to visit that evening was Chenamma's, which was right at the edge of the village. It was a small mud hut where Chenamma and her mother Jayamma stayed, along with her three younger brothers and two younger sisters. Jayamma's mother had been a Jogini and her mother before her. Jayamma had fallen pregnant with Chenamma when she was just sixteen, but had been seriously ill for the last two years, unable to support her family. She and Mansa had been good friends when Mansa was a Jogini. They would often sweep the temple steps together, trying to stay shaded in the heat of the day as they swapped news of their neighbours and complaints of their own hardships.

When Mansa poked her head inside the hut she saw something she had not often seen since her arrival in Agnipatnam, a warm smile. Jayamma came up and wrapped her thin arms around Mansa, planting a kiss on her cheek and leading her into the hut by the hand, her bony fingers interlinked with Mansa's.

Inside, Chenamma was sitting on the dirt floor, her little

brother held tightly in her arms as she sang him softly to sleep. The other children, wearing only shorts, ran around happily chasing the chickens outside of the hut. Jayamma gestured to the single wooden stool for Mansa to take before she squatted on the floor beside her.

As Jayamma began to speak she coughed. A small tickle to begin with, but it soon gathered momentum, like a single rock building to an avalanche. She bent over double, hacking away until eventually she regained control. Clearing her throat she spat a ball of blood on the dirt floor and wiped her mouth with the back of her shaking hand. Mansa stared at her, face lined with worry. Jayamma waved a hand of dismissal.

"It's been like this for at least a year. The blood comes and goes. Some days I feel too weak to even stand." She shook her head. "Enough of this sad talk, tell me everything about you! How is life in the big city? You are much happier, yes?" Mansa nodded, a smile creeping onto her face. Jayamma stared at her, a childlike look on her face at the wonder of being able to leave this place and go somewhere else. Anywhere else. She could not even picture life outside Agnipatnam.

"They treat us well. I have somewhere to stay and the boss is very kind. They have even taught me how to read and write." Jayamma smiled.

"You are so successful and you still come back to see us. Who would have thought that a Jogini would read and write!" She chuckled, but it turned into a cough she buried in her sari. Mansa looked at her, troubled.

"It's not too late for you too. Why don't you come with me now? You could start a new life there. They even have a hospital where they can look after you." Jayamma smiled sadly and shook her head. "I fear I don't have long left. This life here, it is all I have known. My family is here. I know nothing of the city."

"I can teach you. There is a better life just waiting for you, if you will come with me?" Mansa pleaded.

"We are not all as brave as you sister. I could never dream to do what you have. I am just a simple woman, and a scared one at that. I am proud of you though. Look at where you came from and now you can read and write." She stopped as another coughing fit came on, holding a hand out to stop Mansa as she tried to approach and help. As she turned to face Mansa, a line of blood trickled from the corner of her mouth.

"If it's too late for you, then what about Chenamma?" Mansa asked after the coughing subsided. They both looked at the shy girl in the corner humming melodies as she rocked the child in her arms. Mansa's tone became urgent. "Jayamma, you know what they will do to her. She can come with me. I will keep her safe, raise her as if she was my own daughter."

Jayamma took Mansa by the hands, her trembling fingers long and slender.

"My mother was a Jogini, then I was a Jogini. It now falls on my daughter to take up the role. Maybe life will be better for her than it was for us."

"How? Nothing here changes. You know that as well as I do. Why can't she be given the freedom to escape this life? To have a better life than we did."

Jayamma coughed and pointed to the door of the hut where they could hear the screams of delight from the children playing. "I have five other children. I am now no use to anyone. Who will look after them when I am gone? We must trust the goddess."

"She will be paid well in the factory, every month she can send some money home..." Jayamma coughed and held out her hand to quiet Mansa. "She may make some money, but she is needed here to look after her family. Her freedom does not come above her family's survival. We know this life of the Jogini, it is all we can do." Mansa opened her mouth to speak but Jayamma squeezed her hand for silence.

"It is too late now anyway. She has already been promised. If she was to turn her back on the goddess now who knows what would happen? Yellamma is not one to forgive such a thing." At these words she dropped her eyes from Mansa as she realised what she had said. Looking back at her daughter she gently whispered, "This is the path she must walk."

Mansa tried once more to speak but Jayamma waved a hand. "It was good to see you again after all this time, but I must rest now. Goodbye old friend," she said, and curled up into a ball on the floor like a kitten before Mansa could respond.

As Mansa walked towards the home of her sister to find rest for the night, she recounted that conversation in her head, overwhelmed with frustration. She had failed in her mission. If only she was smarter, she may have had the words to convince them. Why couldn't someone else have come? Joshna would have had the words *and* the courage to speak. Everyone listened when *she* was speaking. There must have been something more she could have said to convince them, Mansa thought to herself.

The only thing which brought her strength was the chance to see her beautiful niece and hold her in her arms again after so many years. She would have changed so much Mansa wondered if she would even recognise her. Would she recognise Mansa? Mansa had sent photos but didn't know if they had been received. Her sister was illiterate and she never heard back.

Cutting through the shrubs outside her sister's hut she saw a shadow walking up the path towards her. For a moment she wondered if her sister had come to greet her, but the person was far too short and had a much rounder figure. Waddling towards her, she saw braided dreadlocks of hair swaying from side to side.

Mansa stood rooted to the spot as it became clear to whom the silhouette belonged. She stared in horror as Renuka stepped into the light, a smile on her face. Renuka placed the Jagha on the ground in front of Mansa and then placed her hands on her hips.

"Good to see you again, *Balamma,* " Renuka said, her eyes shining with glee at the horror on Mansa's face. Mansa shook her head as she fought to control her emotions. She tried to push past, but Renuka grabbed her tightly by the arm.

"No, you can't..." Mansa began, trying to wriggle free of Renuka's grip. Renuka laughed, pointing with her free arm to the shadow of Anitha appearing in the doorway of the hut.

"Understand this Balamma. You can run, but you can never escape the goddess."

Chapter 12

Anitha and Mansa

"How could you?" Anitha's auntie was screaming at her mother. She had arrived only a few minutes earlier and had fallen on the floor, weeping hysterically as soon as she entered. A bandage was wrapped around her head with blood soaking the back of it. Anitha wondered if she had been hurt badly and that was what caused her to fall. She had seen a lot of injured people fall over today. Some were so badly hurt they hadn't been able to get up again.

Anitha had seen her auntie walking up the path, though she had not known who she was at the time. She saw Renuka speaking with her, her auntie had screamed and ran towards their hut, so Anitha had darted back inside. As her auntie entered she first of all fell to the ground screaming, then seeing Anitha backing herself against a wall she ran forward, throwing both arms around her and squeezing her tightly as if she was scared Anitha would float away.

Anitha had been terrified. At first she had no idea who this lady was pulling her into an embrace so tightly that it felt like it would crush her. She had covered Anitha's head in kisses, her own face wet from tears as she sobbed hysterically. The look on Anitha's face must have been enough to show her mother how scared she was.

"Get off her Balamma, you're hurting her!" her mother demanded, taking Mansa by the shoulders. It had the opposite effect though. Instead of releasing her, she tightened her hold around her niece as Anitha had seen monkeys do to protect their babies.

"Hurt her? I would never hurt her. What you have done is going to hurt her! Don't you realise what you have done?" she wailed. Anitha was tense, trying to pull away. She didn't understand what was going on, but knew that she would like to be away from here.

"You're going to scare her. Let her go!" For the first time Mansa properly looked at Anitha and saw the panic in her eyes. Slowly she released her grip. Anitha was shaking gently as she backed away.

"I would never hurt you Anitha. You must know that?" Confused, Anitha looked at her mother for what to do or say to this crazy lady.

"Wait outside Anitha. Your auntie and I have a lot we need to talk about," her mother declared, eyes fixed on Mansa. Both women stood rigidly with their fists clenched by their sides.

Anitha could only vaguely remember the last time she had seen her auntie. She would have been only about two years old or so she had figured out from stories which she had heard of her auntie disappearing into the night. She had left them all to start a new life somewhere in the city. Anitha had almost forgotten she existed, it had been so long.

Standing unsteadily, Anitha moved towards the door, her auntie's eyes following her every step while her mother's gaze remained fixed on at her auntie. As soon as she had left the hut the shouting began.

"How could you?" her auntie repeated. "Did you not see everything I went through? The nights I came sobbing to you, the stories I told, did that not mean anything? The things they did to me I can never forget! How could you want that for Anitha?"

"*Want*? When has anything ever come down to *want*? You are the one who does what you want without thinking about the rest of us. It's not like we have much of a choice is it?"

"There is *always* a choice."

"There is *never* a choice for us! How could we survive? We have no money."

"Why didn't you ask me for more money? I don't have much, but anything I have I would happily give to keep her safe. How much do you need?" Her auntie reached inside her sari drawing out a wad of rupee notes. "One hundred? Two hundred?" she asked, trying to force the money into her sister's hand.

"Too much." Her mother pointed to Prabu who lay quietly in the corner. Her eyes dropped to the ground and the fight seemed to go out of her. "Everything we had has been spent on medicine for Prabukumar. Still he grows weaker and weaker every day. We have borrowed lakhs from men outside the village. I had no other way. But still the medicine does not work, he only gets worse. We have tried everything," she said mournfully.

"There must be another way. Give me time, I will find you the money," Mansa begged, taking a step forward. Her sister shook her head.

"It has to be this way. If she becomes a Jogini then the sickness will leave him. That is why the medicine is not working. She will bring blessings to us and heal her brother."

"You know that is a complete lie! There will be no healing and you will have lost *both* your children." The slap her mother delivered caused Anitha to wince as she peered in around the door. It was not enough to stop her auntie though who grew even fiercer. "You would sacrifice her for him?"

"He is my eldest boy. I would do anything to have him safe. If she does not become a Jogini then I will have to find a dowry for her. Where will I get the money for that too? This way she will stay here and she can help look after her brother rather than leaving to her husband's home. My husband is dead, how am I to support them?" She looked at her sister, her eyes narrowed. "How? Tell me if you have all the answers." Anitha's auntie took another step, her voice now quiet, dropped almost to a whisper.

"Let me take her with me. Then you will have no dowry to pay and she will be free to work. She is a clever girl. She can learn to read and write, she will be able to make clothes. Think of how much more she will do than we ever did. She can send home all the money she makes to help Prabukumar."

"And my debts? Will they just forget them? I cannot read and write like you, but I am not stupid enough to think that. What will they do to Prabukumar and me if she leaves? They wanted her. She was the only price they would take."

"You have already promised her?" Anitha's mother only looked at the ground. After a moment she answered softly. "I was told if she was given to them they would forget the debts. It was the only way. If not, they would never leave us alone."

"You know what they will do to her?" Her mother did not look up. Her auntie picked up the tattered bag that she had left on the floor. "I cannot stay here any longer. You are no sister of mine." With that she turned and stormed out of the hut. Anitha ducked her head back outside, frightened to be caught listening.

As her auntie came outside she was sitting on a tree stump near the hut. Mansa crouched down so that she was at eye level with Anitha. Anitha swallowed, fearful of what she would say. She did not want to be shouted at like her mother had been. Instead, her auntie spoke in a soft voice, almost too quiet to hear.

"I will not let this happen. I promise I will stop it." She studied Anitha for a long moment, opening her mouth as if there was more she wished to say, before she stood, kissed Anitha on the head and walked away.

Chapter 13

Rupa

All three of them sat staring blankly at the blinking screens in front of them, trying to think of any other explanation for the death of these three reporters than what seemed to be staring them in the face.

"Maybe it's just some huge coincidence?" Ben said, holding up his palms and wrinkling his nose. The looks he received from Stuart and Rupa persuaded him not to bother saying any more.

"We've got to get out of here," Stuart glumly conceded. "It doesn't sound like these are the kind of guys who mess around."

"Whoa! Hold on dude, let's not be hasty," Ben countered. "Look at what we have already uncovered! We are on to something big here. Think of the story it's going to make! We can't just drive off pretending we haven't seen anything. We can nail these bastards with a bit more research. We've got all this on him after two minutes on Google. Think about what else we might uncover with a bit of time."

"Exactly my point, look where that research got these reporters! I don't want that to be me," he said, pointing at the crumpled car in the story in front of him.

"Come on man, you're overreacting. It's not like he even knows we are on to him. By the time what we make is seen by anyone we will be long gone from here, tucked up safely back in the UK. It will be fine." Stuart's cheeks flushed.

"What if it's not fine Ben? What if he's planning something *right now* after we arrived in the middle of that riot, waving a camera around and filming him hanging a little girl? That doesn't sound like it will work out fine to me. There are already at least three dead reporters at his hand, I don't want to be another one."

"Stuart, calm down man. There are twenty thousand people around. It's not like he would risk anything in the middle of all that. Think of the big picture. Just imagine what a story like this could do for our careers when we get back."

"If we get back at all. It's not some big game Ben, I can't take these sorts of risks, it's not safe."

"If it's safe you're after, why did you get in to this? Why didn't you get a quiet little desk job somewhere?"

"Screw you. You don't have two little girls waiting for you to get home."

"And what about the little girl we saw hanged today? What about *her*?"

"That's low man, really low," he said, standing and pushing past Ben. He slammed the door as he exited and sank down to the floor, leaning against the van in the twilight. When Rupa and Ben came out a few moments later his wallet was open and he was staring at a photo of his wife, Julie, and their twin daughters in matching red hats, golden pigtails spilling out from under them.

Ben looked at Stuart, then at the ground, tracing shapes in the dust with his shoe as he thought what to say. After a moment he sighed.

"I'm sorry man," Ben said, lifting his cap and flattening

the hair under it. "Just this whole thing has got under my skin. Filming it and everything, it kind of screws you up, you know? It was unfair to say that." Stuart looked up at him.

"You got a smoke?" he asked. Ben patted down his pockets and pulled out a near empty packet of Lucky Strikes, offering it to him. Stuart had not smoked since the girls were born nearly seven years ago, but right now it was what he needed to take the edge off. He puffed away as the others stood in silence next to him.

His hands trembled slightly as he placed the wallet back in his pocket. Rupa placed a hand on his shoulder.

"Stuart, unless we are all one hundred per cent happy to stay we can get in that van right now and drive to the nearest town, far away from here and all that we have seen. There is no pressure at all. We can find a different story, maybe head back to the brick factory? We could chat more with Mounika about how the female workers are treated like we were going to do?" They stood there in silence as her words dissipated in the night air. Just as Rupa thought Stuart wasn't going to answer, he looked up at them both, his blue eyes sharp and penetrating.

"I'll stay on two conditions," he stated. "The first is that we get out of here as soon as that Jatara is finished, regardless of what we uncover. The *minute* it's done, ok?" They nodded. "The second," he said as they looked at him intently, "is that you don't tell Julie I was smoking. She would kill me herself." He gave a half smile as Ben chuckled.

"Done." Ben said as he held out an arm and helped him up, before turning to walk back in the van. Stuart continued to stand by the door.

"You asked me why I first got into this." Ben stopped and looked around at him. "To sound like a walking cliché, I wanted to try and make a difference. The first time I saw my girls, it changed me. You start to realise how crap this world can be and I wanted to make it a better place for them, a place they would be safe in which to grow up. I wanted to at least do something that they could be proud of. Maybe this is one of those chances to step up and actually do something. I guess it's a time to be brave." Ben nodded in agreement, then they both headed into the van, continuing the conversation.

Rupa watched them go, the responsibility of choosing to stay in Agnipatnam weighing heavily on her. She waited in the dusk for a moment, searching the shadows to see if anyone was watching, before following them into the van.

Chapter 14

Rupa and Mansa

The village was in darkness apart from a few open fires that were mostly down to embers now in the early hours of the morning. The power had gone off a few hours earlier, everywhere was now calm after the mayhem of the day and weary travellers lay down to sleep by the roadside.

The moonlight shone through the windows of the battered green and red van sitting alone at the edge of the village. Inside, Rupa, Stuart and Ben all sat hunched over their computers, their faces bathed in a dull blue glow. The sound of fingers dancing over the keys was the only noise punctuating the silence. Every now and again one of them would straighten up and read their latest discovery with a grim face.

"There is an article from this Sagar guy in 2010 accusing Chaudhury of intimidation in Dalit villages to either vote for him or not to vote at all. Apparently one of the polling stations in a Dalit village was set on fire during the polls, making all their votes void. Nothing was ever linked to Chaudhury but Sagar is making a lot of noise about it here," Ben observed, as he scanned through the story.

Every article they discovered was like a thread that was joined to another, pulling them ever deeper into the darkness.

"There are some pretty strong accusations here..." Stuart began, when suddenly they heard footsteps crunching on the stones outside as someone ran towards the van. As they looked wild-eyed at each other, fists starting pounding on the closed door and they heard the clicking of the lock as the door was frantically rattled. Ben was quickest to react, grabbing Stuart by the shoulders and pushing him towards the front of the van. "Drive! Go!" Stuart sprang to life, diving over the seats to the steering wheel as the banging intensified. Rupa looked around, quickly grabbing the ashtray from the table, holding it in her hand ready to strike, as Ben grabbed the camera boom pole and pointed it at the door. The handle shook as Stuart fumbled to get the keys in the ignition, before Rupa heard the cry in Telugu from outside. "Help! Please, help!"

"Stuart, wait!" She shouted, suddenly able to breathe again.

"What? There's no time!" he called over his shoulder, turning the keys in the ignition and revving the engine. "Stuart!" she shouted. He turned around and as the banging slowed the boys could also hear a female voice, racked with sobs, crying for help. Breathing a collective sigh of relief, Stuart slumped down in the chair and Ben gingerly placed the boom back on the floor as Rupa unlocked the door and beckoned Mansa inside. As she entered, her eyes were red and swollen and her dishevelled hair clung wildly to her weathered face, sticking up at all angles from below the bandage. Her back was bent as she crouched, pulling her sari tightly around herself.

"Anitha. Anitha. Anitha." That was all they could get from her as she was ushered into a seat by Rupa. Ben looked outside into the darkness to check there was no-one else, then he closed the door and made sure it was locked. Rupa knelt in front of the girl, taking her hands as she waited for Mansa to compose her thoughts.

"Anitha. Jogini," were the only two words she managed to get out, her lips trembling as she spoke.

That was all that was needed for Rupa to comprehend what she was saying as she embraced Mansa and let her weep.

After a moment Mansa pulled away. "The Jatara. Tomorrow. Anitha will be dedicated then handed over to them. She is only eleven! After all that I went through, how could they do that to her?" Rupa shook her head to show her support. Mansa reached out and gently took Rupa's head in her hands. Holding Rupa intently with her eyes she declared "She is all I have. We have to stop this. You must help me."

Chapter 15

Anitha

Her mother was there. She was smiling. So proud, she had never looked happier. The lines of worry that usually creased her face were gone and her eyes sparkled with joy.

She pushed Anitha's hair back and kissed her on the forehead like Anitha always wanted her to do. She began walking around Anitha, wrapping her in a new white sari lined with golden flowers at the edges. It was so beautiful. More beautiful than anything she had ever seen. Her mother carefully folded in the many pleats so that the sari swayed like the waves of the sea when she moved. Anitha gasped in pleasure and clapped her hands together.

Her mother opened a small red box, pulling out the jewellery gifted to Anitha. First she clasped on the golden anklets, tapping them to make the bells jingle. Next she stood and poked the gold earrings into both of Anitha's ears, smiling the whole time. Finally, she reached into the box and drew out the thaali necklace, red thread decorated with white cowry shells which almost seemed to glow in the sunlight. She placed it lovingly over Anitha's head, the shells forming a 'V' shape across her chest. She could feel them rise and fall with every breath she took. Anitha reached up, running her fingers gently over the smooth curves in the shell's surface.

"Just beautiful. Today is your day," her mother said, cupping Anitha's face in her hands to kiss her again, before standing back to admire how she looked. Nodding her approval she smiled before turning to fetch some water from the cracked clay jar in the corner. Anitha stood for a moment, looking down at all her jewels and the stunning sari in which she was dressed, like a girl from a film that Javali had shown her. She spun around, delighted at the feeling of the bells chiming and the sari being spun around her. Holding her arms out she watched as the sunlight played on the sequins, giggling as she seemed to sparkle. For the first time in her life she felt beautiful.

As she span around she felt the shells on her necklace begin to rise up her chest, past her collar bone until they collected around her neck. The red thread became tighter and tighter, making it difficult to breathe. She reached up and grabbed the necklace, but it continued to close around her throat, the shells nipping her skin. In desperation she tried to scream out to her mother, but no sound would leave her lips. The necklace began to cut into her flesh, until she couldn't draw breath. Blood ran between Anitha's finger as she tried to pull it away, but she couldn't make it stop. The room began to spin and as she fell to her knees there was nothing she could do....

It was still dark outside as Anitha woke writhing around on her thin blanket that was soaked through with sweat. It was wrapped around her legs as she kicked to get free. Reaching up she grabbed at her neck, running her hands around it to feel for the necklace, but felt only clammy skin. She then clutched both ears, relieved to find nothing but her naked lobes. Shakily she exhaled and rested her head on her knees, trying to get her breath back.

She placed her hands on her head for comfort, but as she raised them she saw blood smeared on her wrist. She gasped, frantically looking around to see where she was hurt. She wiped her arm and it did not bleed, and she could feel no cut on her face or body but then she became aware of the warm, sticky feeling between her legs. In the moonlight she could see the dark crimson that had stained through her light green pyjama trousers and had left dark spots on her blanket.

It was the second time this had happened to her. On the first time she had felt stomach cramps before it happened, and had woken in the night because of the pain. She had panicked and run to the lake to wash her nightclothes, although they were still marked now. It had gone on for about four days. She thought she must have been ill, but that was weeks ago and nothing had happened since, so she thought she must be better. What did it mean? What would her mother say if she was ill as well as Prabu? She had to be well so that she could go and make him better. Today was her big day. She had to be well for Prabu.

She looked over to her mother who was curled up on the floor, her eyes closed tightly as she breathed gently. Standing quietly, Anitha crept to the door to go and clean herself, praying that her mother wouldn't catch her and hit her. She had been playing once with Javali and had fallen and cut her leg, ripping her trousers. Her mother had beaten her till she cried for ruining her clothes.

Crouching outside the door, she poured the water from the jug and scrubbed the stain on her trousers, but no matter how much water she poured, the dark marks remained as if to accuse her. Despite her hot tears and frantic rubbing, the blood refused to move. It seemed determined to stay and show her guilt.

Hunched over in the dirt she didn't hear her mother approach and look over her shoulder.

"What are you doing?" she demanded, eyes still glazed with sleep.

Startled, Anitha's only response was to shake her head as she clutched the blanket to her chest. Her mother grabbed the damp blanket from Anitha's hands, wrenching it free of her grip. Holding it up, she inspected the marks of blood in the moonlight. Anitha sat trembling, waiting for her mother's reaction, one arm raised to cover her face. However, her mother's eyebrows creased, then relaxed as a look of understanding crossed her face. A slight smile touched the side of her lips.

"I'm sorry mother. Please, it was an accident," Anitha pleaded, her voice quivering.

"It's alright. It means that you are ready. You won't need those old clothes again. Come. Today is your day," she said, tossing the blanket on the ground. "We have lots to do."

Stunned, Anitha picked up the bloodied blanket and followed her mother back inside.

Her mother was right, there was a lot to do. The rising of the sun brought with it the first of her relatives, her mother's oldest sister Suva dressed in an emerald green sari. On entry to the hut, she pinched Anitha's cheeks so hard it felt like they would come off. Then she took Anitha's chin and turned it up to her, forcing a sugary laddu sweet into her mouth. Without saying a word to Anitha she turned and began planning with her mother, complaining that Anitha was still too short and her skin was too dark.

Within minutes the rest of the relatives followed, a slow trickle to begin with, then flooding the small hut with their noise and fussing. Only three or four could fit inside at one time so they all took turns telling Anitha what she should do and how she should speak to others. They told her how she would feel at certain points of the day and important people to speak to. They told her how she must fulfil her duties. No-one asked how she felt though.

The heat and the noise were too much for her in their small hut. She felt trapped, but they would not give her a moments peace or allow her to sit. Every time she glanced at the door there were new faces looking in, pointing at her and offering their thoughts.

There was so much more advice and wisdom to be given and time was short. She felt light-headed, but any thought of food was ruled out until after the ceremony. Her stomach felt like it was full of wriggling snakes anyway and she would not have kept it down. The dream had terrified her, but there was no-one she could tell it to. The only one who would understand was Prabu, but she didn't know if he could even hear her. He had been hot again last night before they slept, murmuring for most of the night.

She tried to make her way across the room to him, but every step brought her face to face with another stern auntie. She glanced at him as he drew short breaths, his chest gently rising and falling. "Soon you will be better, Prabu," she promised in her heart. "I'll be brave for you." Renuka had said that if she performed her duty, Yellamma would heal him. Maybe by tomorrow he would be okay again.

Before she knew what was going on, they were all being ushered out of the house by her grandmother and heading towards the small lake, Anitha being prodded by rough hands to the front of the group. She heard a bleat and looked round to discover an auntie she had only seen a few times pulling a stubborn goat along with them, its neck adorned with a garland of yellow flowers and a marking of turmeric paste on its head.

As they walked, the familiar sound of the drums to signal the morning of the Jatara began from outside the temple. Every beat seemed to go through her, making her heart shake in her chest. A few voices had begun to take up the cry of "Yellamma, Yellamma," a chant which would continue throughout the day.

It was still early when they arrived at the lake, but already its banks were lined with members of the village, mostly young men leaning on each other's shoulders and chewing paan leaf, spitting red juice onto the dry ground. During the monsoon rains, Anitha would come and fill the water buckets from here. The water then was well above her head. On a few occasions Javali had pushed her in, laughing as Anitha had flapped her arms around, spitting out water. Yesterday though, the water had come no higher than her waist.

They stepped down from the bank of the river, small puddles of mud squelching between their toes as they walked towards the centre where the water was deepest. Only her mother and a few aunties came in with her, the rest standing back, not wanting to dirty their best saris with the murky water. As it covered her toes she looked nervously at her mother who nodded for her to go on. With her next step, the anklets she had been gifted disappeared completely beneath the water.

Her auntie held a basket full of rose petals and others held coconut shells filled with turmeric paste. She looked up and saw many of the village standing around watching them enter the water.

"I don't want to do this," she said to her mother, stopping as the water splashed around their knees. She had never come to the river to see the washing ceremony of the Jatara, but she had heard people from the village talking about it and all that went on. Her mother gripped her arm tightly and whispered sharply in her ear, "You must. Think of your brother. This is the only way to save him."

Anitha sighed and managed to wade into the middle of the river, the water lapping at her waist. It made her clothes feel heavy and she wanted to let them pull her down, to sink deep under the water, away from all the eyes that were watching her.

She felt her auntie's rough hands taking her top and try to pull it over her head. Anitha wedged her arms to her sides in protest, drawing a slap from her auntie. Anitha looked at her mother for support, but she just stood, nodding almost imperceptibly, her jaw clenched.

Terrified, Anitha reluctantly lifted her trembling arms above her head, aiding her auntie with the undressing. She closed her eyes, hoping that if she could not see the eyes staring at her somehow they would not see her either. She could feel the sting of hot tears as her top was removed, people watching as her body was exposed.

As soon as her auntie pulled the top off, Anitha quickly crossed her arms over her chest and squatted down in the water so that only her head was visible. The murky water was her only protection against the prying eyes of the men lining the river bank. She sank lower, embracing the security it gave her, until only her eye lids were visible, like a sleeping crocodile.

A moment later she felt something soft brushing her cheek and opened her eyes to see delicate white rose petals falling like the monsoon rain on the muddy surface of the lake. They looked out of place here, too pure and white on the dirty water. They tangled in her hair which was splayed out on the surface of the water and she wished she could take them away with her, somewhere deserving of their beauty.

As she was pulled above the surface of the water by her auntie, she hugged her shoulders and focused all her attention on one of the petals which seemed to hover just above the water, its touch so light as it slowly span and danced. The whole time she watched its movement, trying to block all else from her mind as her mother and auntie lathered her in thick yellow turmeric paste which made her skin burn. They rubbed it into her back, her arms, her front, even on her face, before splashing the water from the lake over her. The whole time she kept her eyes trained on the dancing petal as it twisted and span in the ripples they caused. It was the only way she didn't have to think about this moment and everyone watching her.

After the cleansing was finished, she became aware of movement at the edge of the water. She looked up and saw the priest approaching, dragging the goat behind him as it tried to pull free from its rope. It dug its heels into the soft mud and drew back, bleating wildly. Anitha felt for it. If it were not for Prabu she would have been the same, fighting every inch of the way, but instead she had to surrender herself to this humiliation, fighting the urge to run away and never stop.

She watched as the priest reached to the back of his tunic, grabbed a knife and in one expert motion pulled back the goat's head as he drew the blade across its throat. She gasped as the blood spurted out, the goat suddenly silent as it collapsed to the ground, crimson spilling into the water. The priest straightened up then beckoned to her mother to come join him, blood staining his fingertips.

She didn't know if it was for comfort or to make her move, but her mother put an arm around her shoulders and they walked forward together, Anitha shivering slightly despite the heat on her naked, raw skin. She was glad of her long hair, falling down to her chest and covering some of her body, rose petals still clinging to it.

As they approached, the priest chanted something she could not understand, his voice rising and falling like he was singing a song. His eyes were closed as he waved his right arm around. Her aunties were there to greet her as she came out of the water, wrapping her in the new green and red sari her mother had shown her. As they dressed her she wondered if she would meet who had bought it for her.

Once she was dressed, the priest stood in front of her

continuing to chant, holding out his hand to her mother. She reached in the folds of her sari and drew out her hand, the familiar red thread and white shells dangling from between her fingers.

Anitha's eyes widened and her hands immediately went to her neck. Her dream flashed before her eyes as the priest took it from her mother. He held up both ends of the red thread and tied them around her neck, the shells falling onto her chest, feeling like weights pulling her down. She looked at him in terror as he spoke to those gathered of the significance of tying the thaali. The thread usually used in marriage, instead used to show the Jogini was now married to the temple.

His top was streaked with blood where he had wiped his hands after the sacrifice. Anitha looked at it, mouth open. As he continued speaking Anitha's mother leant over and whispered in her ear.

"Just beautiful. Today is your day." Anitha tried to swallow but couldn't, her mouth completely dry. She lifted a hand and touched one of the shells.

After that the world went black as she fainted.

Chapter 16

Rupa

Rupa was the first awake, the pounding of the drums pulling her from a fitful sleep. She was surprised that she had managed to drift off at all. Every time she closed her eyes all she could see were the bodies of the journalists who had taken a stand and the shadows cast by the men who had killed them. Added to that was the promise she had made to Mansa to try and help rescue Anitha, the responsibility weighing heavily on her tired shoulders.

Bang went the drum. Bang, bang, bang, pause. Bang, bang, bang, pause.

The sun was not long up, but she knew this was going to be one long day. She sat up and stared into the mirror on the side of the van. Her usually immaculate hair was almost as wild as Mansa's and her face was creased from the cushion she had slept on. Under her eyes were black rings and she had light crow's feet appearing. She smiled as she thought of some of the cloaked comments she'd heard about her looks getting her the presenting jobs. If only they could see her now she thought.

Bang, bang, bang, pause. Bang, bang, bang, pause.

"Time to get moving." She shouted at the boys who were both dozing in the front seats of the van. Stuart stretched and cracked his neck while Ben pulled his cap on to gain some control over his unruly curls. They quietly began to pick up their equipment, each moving slowly to delay the inevitable.

"Right, let's get this done," Ben said with hollow enthusiasm as he slung his bag with the spare handheld camera over his shoulder.

Bang, bang, bang, pause. Bang, bang, bang, pause.

The three of them stood for a moment, looking from one to the other to gain strength.

"Who knows, we might get all we need today," Stuart said, "then we won't even have to stay for the whole Jatara."

"Yeah, we might," Rupa replied with little belief.

"It's going to be a great story," Ben said. They nodded, no-one making the first move to the door. A silence settled between them as they listened to the banging of the drums in the distance, the unspoken fears remaining between them until Stuart spoke aloud what they were all thinking.

"They won't, I mean, they wouldn't know that we are on to them would they?"

"No, no. We'll be fine," Ben said quickly, looking at the ground. "They probably don't even know we're here, let alone interested in them."

"We'll be in the editing suite before you know it," Rupa added.

"Right then."

"Right."

"Right."

Taking a deep breath, Rupa swung open the door of the van, the full effect of the noise outside rushing in. Momentarily dazzled by the sunlight, she looked down and then froze, before running back into the van gasping. Ben pushed past her looking at the dusty floor outside. In the dirt were photos of the three deceased journalists held down by stones, a red cross struck through each face. Ben and Stuart looked at each other wide-eyed.

Bang, bang, bang.

Chapter 17

Mansa and Anitha

The sun had risen far too soon, bringing with it the madness of the day's preparations. Already the streets were full, stalls being erected selling fruit, flowers and small shrines of Yellamma. Amid the bustle there was a carnival atmosphere, the previous day's horrors seemingly forgotten with the dawn of a new day. Chai-sellers meandered through the crowd, silver urns resting on their shoulders, while people snacked on delicious hot samosas and fluffy steamed idli with spicy peanut chutney served on green banana leaves. Young and old went about their rituals, bringing themselves to worship before the goddess, but despite the pious acts few hearts thought only of devotion to the deity. The village fell under the shadow of the tree on the hill, the noose removed but the emotion raw. Villagers with cuts and bruises served as a constant reminder of the unspoken hurt, pain and resentment just beneath the joyful exterior facade of the day.

Mansa had to fight against this crowd as she headed to the river, knowing that they would be bathing the Joginis there before the rest of the ceremony took place later. The riverbanks were packed with onlookers, many of whom were now making their own way into the water to bathe before making their offerings. She scanned the water which was full of groups of boisterous teenagers splashing and pushing each under, amid solemn individuals preparing themselves for acts of devotion. Eventually she sighted Anitha at the side of the lake, surrounded by family members fussing over her and pulling at her sari to straighten it.

Mansa knew there was no way that they would let her get near enough to speak with Anitha. As soon as they saw her approach she would be driven away like a rabid dog. Her only hope was to stick close to them and try and grab an opportune moment, though she knew they were unlikely to let Anitha out of their sight.

She watched the group from a safe distance as they began to meander into the steady throng of people heading towards the temple. After a moment she saw an older Jogini approaching them, the group parting to let her through to speak with Anitha. She gave Anitha prashad food which had been offered to the goddess, then waved a finger as she gave advice and spoke briefly of the duties Anitha was now to fulfil.

Mansa remembered her first and second pattam, the details vivid, even many years on. The first pattam, when she was dedicated to the temple, took place when she was only thirteen. In the few days before the celebration she had been kept inside their hut, unable to leave, but constantly fed jalebi and other sweet treats.

On the morning of the procession she was put at the front of the line, many of the village parading behind her as she carried a brass pot filled with water from the river. She didn't know what was happening, with no-one speaking to her or answering any questions. She was forced to wear nothing but a covering of neem leaves around her privates, and was made to run around the temple three times while carrying the pot atop her head as water spilled over the top, soaking her. Terrified, she was relieved that several other girls were also following the same ritual so she was not alone. The same fear filled their eyes, some of them far younger than her.

Once they had run around the temple the priest had spread out an orange blanket and decorated it with bananas, coconuts and wild flowers, beckoning Mansa, or Balamma as she was then, to sit in the centre. Exhausted and shaking, she sat bewildered as the priest made offerings and threw rice grains on her head. He then tied the thaali thread around her, before placing another necklace with a graven image of Yellamma over her head. That was her wedding day. Her marriage to the temple.

She could still feel the nerves in her stomach from that day. Just being here brought the old emotions rushing back.

She was then paraded at a Jatara when she was fourteen. She recalled the words passed on to her by an older Jogini as she approached the temple. "You are now the goddess. She lives in you," one had said, the sickly sweet smell of alcohol almost overcoming Mansa as the woman leant in close, her lips tickling Mansa's ear. "You must make the goddess happy. You must do all you are told," another had said, her eyes stern as she fed Mansa rice offered to Yellamma.

That had been the night when her innocence was taken from her. Amidst the bustle of the crowd she had suffered grabbing and squeezing as she tried to circle the temple and perform her duty of prayers.

Upset by the groping, she was in tears near the temple gates when one of the local priests had escorted her away from there. Relieved, she thought he was taking her to safety until he led her into a field of cotton next to the temple. Despite her screams, he ripped off her sari and forced himself on her till his appetite was satisfied. He then rolled off her, tied up his white dhothi and walked back to the temple without giving her a second glance.

Before then she had been too naïve to understand exactly what was happening when the men came to visit her mother. There was only one room in their hut, and when visitors came her mother would tell her to take her little sister out to collect water or to visit an auntie. They were best friends as well as sisters back then and would tell each other everything. They would play out for hours; throwing stones, climbing trees or just telling stories.

One day though her sister had fallen and hurt her arm, so Mansa had run back home to get their mother. She ran straight into their hut to find her mother and one of the elders of the village naked on the floor. It sounded like he was hurting her so Mansa called out, but that made them both angry. The elder leapt up and struck her on the back as she turned to run away, chasing her out of the hut even though he was naked.

That night, when she knew the elder had gone, she crept home, checking it was safe before her sister came in. Her mother was still angry with her and said that she had disturbed the work of the goddess so Yellamma would be angry with her. Maybe she would be punished. At the time it made no sense to her what had been happening, but after the evening in the cotton field it all became horribly clear.

After her dedication she was expected to pass on blessings and wisdom to the younger girls, but she just wanted to warn them what life was to become. While everyone else carried on, readily going into trances and performing their duties, she just felt a dark emptiness. If there was a goddess she certainly didn't feel part of her. She tried telling her mother once, but she was horrified and called Mansa proud and wicked, saying that she must have an evil spirit in her. She had to beg her mother not to take her to the priest to remove the spirit. After that she just pretended as best she could, placidly carrying out the rituals and trying to do what was expected, hoping no-one would sense her imitation of conversing with the goddess.

Watching the older Jogini talking with Anitha she wanted to tell her the whispered words were poison, that they were empty and hollow, but there was no way to get to her.

As she stood on the riverbank fuming, a white haired Jogini arrived next to her and placed down her begging bowl, removing her necklaces as she went to wash in the lake. Mansa looked down at them, a slight smile playing on her face. Covering her head with part of her sari, she picked up the necklaces and put them on, shuddering as she saw the familiar cowry shells back around her neck. She grabbed the wooden begging-bowl, empty but for a few rupees and stole a glance to see the Jogini with her back to Mansa, fully immersing herself under the water. Muttering an apology Mansa turned and disappeared into the crowd, being sure to keep her face covered as she huddled over and hurried after Anitha. Begging-bowl held out, necklaces dangling, Mansa felt like she was in a vision of what the future would have held for her if she had not been set free, the future she had to stop Anitha from experiencing.

As she pushed through the crowd she recognised members of the family she had not seen or spoken to since she left the community. She pulled the sari tightly around her head to avoid recognition as she huddled over, changing her walk to a shuffle. Reverence for the necklaces gave her a clear path to Anitha who looked terrified amid the revelry, clutching anxiously at the thread around her neck.

Mansa saw her moment, and as she stood before Anitha she deliberately dropped the begging bowl, a few silver rupee coins rolling out at Anitha's feet. Nobody paid any heed to the foolish old Jogini as she bent low to gather the coins. As Anitha saw the coins by her feet and scrabbled in the dust to help, Mansa reached out her arm taking Anitha's hand in her own. Anitha looked up at her and Mansa loosened the veil so that she could be recognised.

"Mansa Auntie?" she asked, confused. Mansa's eyes darted around; checking no-one had seen her as she readjusted the material.

"Anitha, you can't do this. They will *hurt* you." Anitha's hand automatically reached to her neck, fiddling with the shells around it. "I know the life of a Jogini. It is one I cannot wish on you. Please, don't do it." Anitha looked around, her eyes full of fear.

"I must. Mother has said. For Prabu. If I don't, he will not get better."

"Those are all lies!" Mansa hissed. "It makes no difference

to Prabu. You can't save him by becoming a Jogini. That's just what they want you to think. Please, trust me, you don't have to do this."

"But, Mother said that I have to. The fever is my fault, I must make it right."

"You are not to blame, child. This is not your fault. Please Anitha, listen to me. There is another way, a better way. Come with me. I can take you to another life far away from here."

"But what about Mother and Prabu? Everything I have is here. I can't just leave them and my home."

"It will no longer be home. After tonight everything will be different. Please Anitha, come with me," she said, her grip on Anitha's hand tightening as tears began to well in her eyes.

"Mother won't let them hurt me. She will protect me. I have to stay." With that Anitha made to stand up, but Mansa pulled her down.

"Did she protect you earlier when they took your clothes in the river?" Anitha's cheeks coloured as she remembered the humiliation.

"You cannot trust them. Not one of them. You will see what they will do to you. When you have seen, then you will know that I'm speaking the truth. I will be waiting for you. Do you know the big banyan tree at the back of the temple?" Anitha thought for a moment and nodded. "I know a space where all the roots tangle and you can climb inside, then there's a little space to hide. Have you been there?" Anitha nodded. Sometimes she and Javali used to sit in there and share stories when it was too hot in the sun. It was just big enough for two people, hidden away in the ground under the roots, making it cool. "I will wait there till you come. No matter how long it takes I will wait for you. I will wait forever if I have to." Anitha opened her mouth to speak, then gave a tiny nod before standing and hurrying to catch up with her mother.

Chapter 18

Rupa

"Oh man! This is not good. This is really not good!" Stuart said. Ben knelt down and picked up all three photos struck through with a red cross, holding each up for inspection. Rupa was back inside the van, failing to get reception for her phone to contact the main office back in London.

"Subtle, very subtle," Ben said, waving the photos in front of him. "All the connotations of a horse's head without all the mess. Ten out of ten for style at least," he flippantly remarked, his face pale. He pulled out a cigarette, his fingers trembling slightly as he tucked the photos into his shirt pocket, not wanting to look at them any longer.

"What have we got into?" Stuart asked, his eyes darting from side to side as he checked for anyone approaching the van. He tucked his hands into his arm pits and rocked slightly on his heels as he muttered under his breath. Ben rubbed his eyes and looked around nervously.

After a moment, the van door opened and Rupa walked back out, shaking slightly, the phone still in her hand.

"I can't get hold of the office. We need to get out of here. Hyderabad is the nearest city. We can get there, gather our thoughts and think of a new angle on all this. Stuart, are you OK to drive?" He nodded, the van keys ready between his fingers.

"Hang on," Ben said gently, putting a hand on Stuart's shoulder. "Doesn't this prove we are *right*? That we are on to something?" he asked in a low voice. Rupa and Stuart looked at each other anxiously. "Don't get me wrong. I'm terrified too, but this feels like something we have to follow. Like you said last night Stuart, it's a time to be brave." Stuart looked at him for a moment then tucked the keys back in his pocket.

"Ok, I'm still in. Let's get going before I have a chance to actually think sensibly about this and change my mind." Ben looked at Rupa for confirmation. She held up her hands in a show of defeat.

"Let's do it."

As a precaution, they started the van and meandered slowly through the dust for a few miles, parking up next to a field of shrivelled sugar-cane. Surprisingly it started first time, with only the odd noise to worry about. Revellers banged on the side as they made their way through, some dancing in front of the van, oblivious to the blasts of the horn. Others walked alongside the vehicle for the whole journey, faces animated as they peered through the windows with curiosity. They had thought it may give slightly more anonymity moving away from the celebrations, but it had only served to draw even more attention to them with their dancing entourage.

Rupa placed a hand on Stuart's shoulder as they arrived at an area slightly sheltered by trees. "This is going to be as good as anywhere with our little procession. May as well leave it here. Just make sure that door is locked and take anything you need with you. Who knows if it will still be here when we get back."

Ben put yesterday's tape into the bag with the handheld

camera and Stuart grabbed the boom as they stepped from the van into the mayhem of the Jatara. As predicted, it was an assault on the senses. Within seconds, people were tugging at their shirts, intrigued by their presence and equipment. Stuart had to yank the boom back from a young man intent on stroking it while Ben hugged the camera closely to his chest.

Amid the crowds, people were dancing and drinking, many carrying yellow pots on their heads which were full of food. Music blared out from the temple, with prayers intermittently being chanted over the sound system. The smell of smoke and spices filled the air. Ben looked at the fear etched on Stuart's face and patted him on the back. "Don't worry. It's all going to be fine."

They managed to flow with the crowd which was heading in the direction of the temple, keeping their equipment tightly in hand. As they got near enough, Rupa pointed to Ben and he began to film, first of all taking in the sight of the temple. The walls were a dusty red colour and at least four or five feet thick. They were crumbling now, but once they must have stood an impressive sight for any visitors. Next to the temple was a huge tree, different to any Ben had seen before, its twisted branches curling and flowing back into the ground. Rupa saw him filming it and shouted over the noise, "That's a banyan tree. Its branches come down and form new roots. They grow absolutely huge. I once saw one two hundred feet wide."

They continued toward the temple, every step becoming more difficult as the press of people grew ever tighter. In front of them Ben saw a lady wailing, and every few feet she stopped to prostrate herself on the ground before continuing with her cries. Across her forehead were three yellow stripes and the red bindi dot, which he recognised as the marks of the Jogini. He zoomed in, catching her show of what he assumed was repentance.

All around them the devotees entered the temple carrying coconuts and flowers to give as gifts, each leaving with a red bindi mark on their foreheads. Many crouched on the ground outside, pouring food into neem leaves, then cracking a coconut and offering it to the priests at the gates of the temple.

It was still early but the arid ground around the temple was already becoming saturated with blood from the large number of sacrifices being made. Amid the coming and goings, Rupa noticed a girl of no more than ten, her small arm being held by the liver-spotted hand of a man around sixty. A bare chested priest stood between them tying their scarves together as he chanted. Rupa gestured to Ben who zoomed in to catch the events.

"What's going on there?" Stuart asked, shouting to Rupa to be heard over the crowd.

"Must be a child marriage," she responded, her jaw clenched. "Mansa said they are getting more common in the Jataras to cover up the Jogini dedications. Priests can get in trouble for doing the dedication ceremony now so they marry off the girl to an older man, sometimes from the girl's own family. When he no longer wants her she is then used by the men in the village. Ben, make sure you catch all this," she yelled. Ben nodded his assent, catching the girl being fed a round sweet by the man as she avoided looking him in the eye.

Their filming was suddenly disturbed by another priest though. He stormed towards them, angrily flailing his arms as a gold chain bounced on his chest.

"Stop! You are not to be filming here!" he yelled in Telegu, his bushy eyebrows furrowed.

"Why not?" Rupa responded. "We want to see these marriages and what is happening. We have as much right as anyone to be here."

"Out!" he shouted, furious at being challenged by a woman. Ben and Stuart looked to her for direction. Rupa decided that if they were to get anything useful she had to change her approach. She motioned with her hand for Ben to lower to camera to prevent looking as intrusive.

"I'm sorry Ji," she said as a mark of respect. "My team and I are very interested in the goddess Yellamma and her servants the Joginis, and we wondered if you, as a wise and learned man, could tell us more about their history? We would love to learn." He stood for a moment with his arms crossed, weighing them up.

"I'm not meant to let you film," he said, his tone softened, an air of uncertainty in it.

"Who has told you not to let us film, Ji?" Rupa asked gently. He looked around then shook his head.

"You must go," he said, although his voice now lacked the earlier conviction.

"OK, we don't want to cause you any problems. But before we go, can you please tell us a little about the magnificent temple," she asked, pointing behind them. His eyes darted around. "When was it built?" Rupa asked.

"Many years ago, around the 10th Century." She nodded, gesturing for Ben to start discreetly filming again.

"And how many years have you served here?" He stood a little straighter, chest out. "For twenty years. My father was here before me, and his father before that."

"And what about the Joginis? Have they always served at the temples?"

"For as long back as we can remember. They used to dance before kings. They were some of the most treasured people in the kingdoms."

"And what about now? Are they still treasured?"

"Yes. They are vessels through which Yellamma speaks. It is a very high honour."

"But what about the sexual acts? How does that honour them?" He shuffled on his feet defensively.

"This is an act of union allowing people to connect with the goddess."

"But these are just young girls who are dedicated. They have no choice about what will happen to them."

"No-one is forced into it. They always have a choice," he responded, his temper beginning to rise. "Nobody makes the girls get dedicated."

"How is it decided who will become a Jogini?"

"Yellamma calls some through their dreams. At other times, if she rescues them as a child from terrible diseases, they want to serve her. Many families have served for generations too and their daughters want to serve as their mothers did. We force no-one to be a Jogini," he said, crossing his hands to show his sincerity.

"What about you? Have you ever *visited* the girls?" Rupa probed. He held up a hand.

"This is enough! I have told you that you are not allowed to film here."

"How many dedications have you performed this year?" Rupa persisted.

"None. It is now illegal because of people like you interfering with the work of the goddess," he said, his body tensing. "The dedications no longer happen here."

"What about the girls today? Those taking part in their second pattam? The Night of the Girl Virgin?" Rupa asked, moving closer as she goaded him. The priest turned and shouted at Ben to stop the camera, waving a threatening finger. There was a sudden commotion though, as the crowd pushed into them. They looked and saw everyone parting as a large black BMW rolled smoothly along. The priest spotted it and melted back into the crowd without another word.

It stopped a hundred yards or so from the temple, a well-dressed young man of twenty leaping out to open the back door. Out stepped Chaudhury, straightening himself and dusting down his white shirt while his silver hair sparkled in the sunshine. Ben zoomed in catching the steely look in his eye as he glared at the camera.

"Time to go," Ben announced.

Chapter 19

Anitha

Anitha was handed a clear plastic bottle.

"Drink!" Renuka demanded, her green eye roaming as she pushed the bottle into Anitha's hand. "It will help you become the goddess so that you can see what is to come." Anitha sniffed at the bottle and had to turn her nose away as it made her nostrils tingle.

"What is it?" she asked timidly.

"Joginis are not to ask questions, only to do as they are told. Now drink," Renuka said again roughly. Anitha looked at her mother and aunties but they impatiently nodded their approval. She put the bottle to her mouth and took a sip, the clear liquid burning all the way from her lips, down the back of her throat and into her chest. The heat was too much, and she tried to spit out what was left in her mouth but Renuka forced the bottle back to her lips. "Again, this time no spitting. You must swallow it all."

"But it burns, it hurt me," Anitha said through numb lips, wiping her mouth with the back of her hand. Renuka slapped her hard across the face making Anitha gasp.

"You are not to answer back. You are now the goddess. You are strong. You must drink. A Jogini never complains." Renuka pushed the drink up to Anitha's lips and this time she was forced to drink until it filled her mouth and the alcohol ran down her chin, spilling onto her sari. She grimaced as she swallowed, then began to cough, crouching over as the heat burned.

Worse than the heat though was the cool indifference of those who stood watching, apparently unconcerned by her pain. She looked at her mother, eyes pleading to make it stop, but her mother remained silent, looking at Anitha and waiting for her to continue drinking.

"More," Renuka said handing it to her and raising her hand to hurry her. "You will see what is to come. The goddess must see the future. They will ask to know. They must know," she said. Anitha was about to ask who *they* were but was forced to take the bottle once more. This time the burn was less and after a short while her fingers began to tingle. The colours around her seemed brighter somehow and the shouting of the crowd seemed like it was no longer close but coming from somewhere far away. Her cheeks began to feel warm and her head was beginning to feel like it had been stuffed with rice. She suddenly had the urge to sit, to close her eyes for a moment and rest, but Renuka was still in front of her, speaking and giving more orders. She tried to focus, and saw that in Renuka's hand was now a headless plucked chicken. Anitha had no idea where it had come from but watched bemused as Renuka took the bird and threw it on the ground by their feet. Crouching down she began to mix the bloody chicken in the mud, slapping it hard in the dirt. Soon it was covered and Renuka straightened up holding the meat between her fingers. She held it out to Anitha, her eyes solemn.

"Eat!" she demanded. Anitha looked at it, the smell of the raw meat almost making her sick. She took it in both hands then looked at her mother who nodded. Timidly she took a small bite, the dirt filling her mouth and crunching between her teeth as tried to chew through the rubbery meat that felt like it was wriggling in her mouth. As she chewed, the mud stuck to her teeth and mixed with her saliva, spilling out the corner of her mouth.

"More," Renuka demanded. Anitha tried to look at her and plead for it to stop, but everything before her was beginning to spin. She looked for her mother but couldn't see her among the blur of colours. The chicken slipped from her hand and she stumbled forwards, dropping to her knees.

Anitha closed her eyes to try and stop the spinning, putting her hands over her ears to block out the world. Within a moment though, she felt her head pushed backward as more of the horrible drink was poured down her throat, mixing with the mud in her mouth as she tried to swallow. It caught in her throat and she retched, the liquid coming straight out. She bent over in the dirt, coughing as she was sick again and again, the bile stinging the back of her nose and making her eyes water. The acidic smell was overpowering as her head hung limp above the mess, a line of dribble hanging from her trembling lips as she muttered for them to stop.

She just wanted to be left alone but somebody was pulling at her, grabbing the top of her arms. Then there were more hands, she had no idea how many, pushing and pulling. Anitha was hoisted to her feet by them all and then carried along in the crowd before the arms released her and she crumpled on the ground.

It was quieter here away from the beating of the drums and she could feel a slight breeze on her face. She closed her eyes and tried to breathe deeply. Her stomach was still churning and she was finding it difficult to swallow. She couldn't be ill, not now. It was her big day. She had to be strong and make Prabu well again. It was the only way. She had to please them all to make Prabu better.

She opened her eyes and looked around. Her mother was not far away, and she stood watching three women dancing through the crowd. Anitha opened her mouth to call out, then noticed an older woman sat near her, rocking back and forth. The whites of her eyes were showing and she was saying something quietly under her breath. Anitha watched her for a while. After a moment, the whispering became louder and the lady began to shout "Yellamma" over and over as she stretched out her hands towards the temple.

Anitha sat and watched her, trying to focus on the lady as the world continued to spin. From the corner of her eye she saw Renuka approaching. It seemed like there was more than one of her, each of them whirling round and surrounding Anitha as they came closer. She weakly held up her hand to ask for no more, but the number of fingers she held up kept seeming to change, more spinning out from her hand. The gold on her sari seemed as bright as the sun as it hung over her arm, and the bangles on her wrist seemed to glow. Renuka slapped Anitha's hand away as she approached.

"You are now the goddess, you must perform the trance." Anitha opened her mouth to respond, but her tongue felt too thick to speak. She saw Renuka scowling so she pushed herself into a crouch and began to rock backwards and forwards mimicking the old lady. Her eyes felt heavy so she closed them and started to mutter "Yellamma" beneath her breath, hoping to please Renuka. If she could look like she was trying, then maybe they would make Prabu better.

After a few moments she forgot that anyone else was there. She kept rocking, the feeling soothing her as she began to drift into oblivion. She began to forget everything that was going on around her. All of the sights and sounds were tuned out.

Anitha screwed her eyes tightly together and she saw swirls of colour shooting across her eyelids; greens, reds and purples all mixing together. They moved around, chasing each other until they formed together into an image of the temple before her. As she watched, bright flames began to fall from the sky, landing on the temple and making it leap with fire. The flames twisted and moved, assembling as the mouth of a giant horrible monster which opened its jaws and began to consume everything around it. People ran away screaming as stalls of sweets were devoured whole.

Inside the temple she saw something moving. Peering closely, she saw Renuka, her thick hair ablaze as she tried frantically to beat out the fire. Debris from the temple was falling all about her as she looked around, full of fear. The walls crumbled down and the roof toppled in, Renuka disappearing below it.

Then she saw her Auntie Mansa waiting for her by the Banyan tree. She was trying to scramble out from among its roots, but already the fire was leaping up the tree. The roots were twisting as if they were alive, and forming a prison to hold her in as the fire spread, surrounding its gigantic trunk.

She pushed the roots trying to fight, but they grabbed her arms and legs, pinning her to the ground as black smoke covered her from Anitha's view. Anitha screamed out for it to stop, powerless to do anything.

The monster of fire began to laugh, its mouth wide as it cackled, spitting flames out from its throat. Anitha stood and watched, trying to think how to stop it, when she realised there was something familiar about it. It took a moment, but then as the flames twisted and meshed together, she made out a human face. One she had seen only yesterday as Javali was dragged away. The politician with the silver hair, nodding by the tree.

She watched in horror as people ran away, but he breathed after them, the heat consuming all. Then his eyes locked on her and she could see the smile widen in his fiery jaws. With a burning tongue he licked his flaming lips then opened his mouth, ready to consume her.

Anitha woke on her back, throwing her arms and legs around wildly as she screamed 'fire' over and over, her sari soaked with sweat. Her mother was crouched at her side telling her to be quiet as she tried to hold her arms down.

"The fire, the fire is coming!" Anitha screamed out, looking around wild-eyed to see what was happening. "I saw it; it will come for us all. No-one is safe. We must leave!"

"There is no fire Anitha. You must be quiet, you will scare people," her mother said firmly.

"But the fire, it was there," she said confused, pointing down to where the crowds were continuing in their merriment.

"It was just a dream. Look, nothing has happened. Now you must come with me. There is something you must do."

"But you must believe me. I saw the fire. Everywhere, we have to get away. It was more than a dream," she pleaded, taking hold of her mother's arms as she struggled to sit. "Where is Renuka? She will know what to do."

"She has gone to make sacrifices."

"I must warn her. Where did she go?" Anitha asked.

"To the temple."

Chapter 20

Mansa

She had to reach the tree. If Anitha arrived, she must be there waiting for her. She couldn't let her down. Not now.

Mansa pulled the worn shawl tighter around her face as she pushed on, dragging herself through the crowd. The Jogini necklaces weighed heavily around her neck but she knew that she couldn't just discard her outfit when surrounded by so many people. She kept up the charade, bent over as she thrust the begging bowl in front of her, edging ever closer to the tree at the back of the temple.

The festivities were becoming more animated as the day wore on, the crowd full of merriment as she made her way through it. In front of her several young Jogini were dancing, the crowd cheering as they stamped their feet, the girl's eyes glazed. She tried to get past, but everyone was too tightly pressed for her to squeeze through. The girls were not much older than the one she had seen hanged yesterday, Mansa thought, shivering at the images forever burned into her mind. Stopped still, she was forced to watch as the girls were paraded through the crowd, drunken men laughing as they reached out and groped at the girl's arms, legs and buttocks as they passed.

She pulled the shawl tightly around her shoulders, trying to suppress the rage she felt burning within her. How could the girl have been killed for polluting the upper-caste boy, yet here it was fine to touch, grab and use the Jogini however anyone wanted? How was this upholding the purity of the community? She bit her tongue to keep from yelling at the hypocrisy, and forced herself to exhale deeply.

Mansa could feel the familiar red mist coming on which has caused her problems in the past. There was no time for it now though. She had to think only of Anitha. If she let it take her over, she would be lost. Who knew what would happen to her, and she wouldn't be able to get to the tree for Anitha. She had to remain calm. Deep breaths like Anna Ma'am had taught her. She searched through her memories for a prayer she had been taught at the factory, grabbing hold of it to strengthen her. It was painted on an old wooden board and hung on the wall behind Anna Ma'am's desk.

"God, grant me the serenity to accept the things I cannot change, the courage to change the things I can, and wisdom to know the difference."

Serenity Mansa. Now is the time for serenity, she whispered to reprimand herself.

As the procession of girls passed, the crowd stumbled forward to fill the gaps they had left. Men filed after them, stepping in time to the beat of the drums as they laughed, arms thrown around each others' shoulders. Mansa stood and watched them for a moment with disgust, her eyes narrowed. As they passed, one of the men fell onto her, causing the begging-bowl to slip out of her hands. Cursing, she knelt down, cautiously feeling between the striding legs to retrieve it. Legs stamped in the dirt, the bowl being kicked forward by careless feet. She scrambled after it on all fours, before becoming aware that she had crawled into the middle of a group in a heated discussion.

"Kalluri Sir won't like that. He has already said that we are bringing too much attention to ourselves after yesterday," one man said, his tone defensive.

"And you don't think they will bring *more* attention if they carry on?" another sneered, the whip in his voice familiar to Mansa. "Do you think it's a coincidence they are here just before the election?" She continued collecting the small coins from between their feet, completely ignored by the men towering over her.

"I don't know, I'm just passing on what Mr Kalluri told me. He's not happy with what's been going on here and he definitely will not be happy with this."

"Well, he's not here now, is he? So I'm the one you have to listen to. If it wasn't for *me*, he wouldn't be Chief Minister anyway, that's something he seems to have forgotten." Mansa peeked up to see the familiar face of Chaudhury standing over her in his immaculate white shirt, his fists balled as he responded. Mansa gasped, dropping the bowl and sending the coins flying once more. The wooden bowl rolled forward, stopping against Chaudhury's foot. He looked down and immediately she did the same, being sure to keep her face covered to avoid recognition. He tutted, angry at the interruption.

"This is exactly what I mean. Look at this useless old woman. If she was an animal, someone would have put her out of her misery by now. She can't even hold a bowl in her hands without shaking. Kalluri has been too weak with these Dalit dogs. They respond to strength, not words. He has brought this problem on himself and us. The Dalits have been allowed to speak when they should have been crushed like the vermin they are!" he said, putting his boot in Mansa's side and kicking her over with his heel.

She yelped as she landed in the dirt.

"Have you no respect for the Joginis?" Someone responded angrily, stepping forward.

"They are dogs, Kuldeep, so *no*, I don't have any respect for them. They are given far too much prestige. Kalluri has allowed them, and all these filthy Dalits, to begin to see themselves as the same as us. They have to know their place. There is a natural order, and they are at the bottom," he said looking down and booting Mansa's bowl into the crowd. She heard a muttered agreement from most of the group above her. Keeping her head lowered she began to crawl out from the huddle, being sure not to make eye contact and draw more derision, a skill she had learned over the years.

"And that is what we must do with this camera crew too," he continued. Mansa paused, paralysed by fear.

"If we just let them come in and say what they want, who knows what lies they will spread about us? We have fought too hard for too long to have these outsiders come in and ruin our work. We have already sent them a warning, but it appears they have foolishly chosen to ignore it." More mutters of agreement, though there were still dissenters willing to voice their concerns.

"These are not local reporters we can buy off for a lakh of rupees."

"Buy off? I didn't mention money. I said we need to show

them their place. We must deal with them. Now!" Chaudhury said, pumping his fist in his hand.

"But, Kalluri will..."

"Did I ask you to speak Kuldeep? They need sorting, and *right now* before the problem gets worse. And if you don't want sorting too I suggest you get on your way. If Kalluri has any problems, tell him to come and see me. He knows where I will be tonight." He paused, looking down at Mansa who was as still as a statue, hunched between two of the men, her head turned to the ground. "What is she still doing here? You see, this is what happens when you allow the dogs to roam as they please. They lose all respect for their masters. When that happens, well, it's only a matter of time   before they bite the hand that feeds them. I'm not going to let that happen, even if Kalluri seems intent on it. You see, they respond only to this," he said, bringing a hand sharply down across her back. Mansa yelped and turned to flee, stumbling into the crowd as one of the group clipped her heels.

She pushed through the crowd hoping to warn them. But even in her panic, one thought swept all others aside. Anitha. She stood still for a moment thinking what to do, then made her decision, praying for forgiveness as she did so.

Chapter 21

Rupa

"Not to be funny, but I was just wondering, what exactly is the plan here?" Ben shouted to Rupa, who was cutting through the crowd ahead of him.

"Right now it's getting ourselves as far as we can from Chaudhury and his henchmen. In the long term, I have no idea," she shouted back over her shoulder.

"That's comforting, just wanted to be sure," he called after her, while forcing his way through a group of men passing a bottle between them.

Stuart lagged behind, only just managing to keep sight of Ben's red baseball cap bouncing through the crowd as he struggled to manoeuvre the sound-boom through the throng. Just as he got closer to them, someone would dance through, separating them once more. Every tug at his shirt caused him to fearfully look around, expecting trouble. He gripped the boom tightly in case he needed to wield it in defence. It felt exposed here at the back, an easy target if anyone was after them.

Stuart was relieved when a few minutes later he saw Rupa and Ben emerging from the crowd. He follow shortly after, heading up a steep hill, past a crumpled gold painted statue of Gandhi which was missing an arm. There were a few trees dotted around here, and people were much less densely packed. Some groups sat around talking as they watched the festivities unfolding below them. The effects of the alcohol had caught up with others who lay flat out on their backs, empty bottles strewn around them as they slept off the worst of it in the heat of the midday sun.

Rupa was flushed in the cheeks and struggling to catch her breath as they gathered under the statue in the small shade that it offered.

"So," she said, hands in the small of her back as she straightened up. "It would seem that Chaudhury has put in an appearance. Kalluri, well, who knows if he is here or not? We know that he will be later though, with his big speech coming up. For now, we somehow need to get as close to Chaudhury as we can and get some sort of evidence that is going to incriminate him. Any ideas?"

"He knows we're here. If we try and get close, he's either going to be on his best behaviour so we don't get anything or his guard dogs are going to chase us off," Stuart said miserably.

"No, that bastard is bound to do something shady. It's in his nature, look at what he did to us this morning with the pictures. We just need to catch him. I say we try and stay covered in the crowd and film him until he does something," Ben said energised.

"Ben, look at us, we're not exactly going to blend into the crowd are we?" Stuart responded.

"Yeah, well, what's the point in us sticking around if we just hide from him? We might as well head home and have a decent bed to sleep in. We have to do *something*."

"There's a difference between doing something and just getting ourselves beaten up, or worse," Stuart retorted.

"Alright, alright," Rupa said, holding her hands out to pacify them. "I say we try and grab some footage and interviews about these Joginis, lay low for a little while then in a bit when he relaxes we get a bit closer, get the zoom on full and see what he is up to from a decent distance. What do you say?"

"I've got nothing better," Stuart said. Ben shrugged, then crossed his arms, "might work, I guess."

They took a moment to set up, and then Ben zoomed out to film the scene below of the whole village. From up here it was possible to get a bit more scale on the size of the Jatara. It was absolutely huge. The temple sat proudly in the middle of it all, people marching in and out like ants to an anthill. From the outside of the village there were still people streaming in, compressing those already struggling for space in the centre.

The women's saris were a sea of colour; the reds, pinks, greens and yellows all mixing and flowing together as people danced excitedly. Every so often a firework would rip out of the crowd, exploding like a flare above the restless ocean of humanity. Screams and shouts echoed up to them between the beats of the drum.

The hillside felt like a tranquil place compared to the mayhem below. Ben turned the camera around, swooping across the immediate scene next to them. People were more scattered here, a few sat in trance-like states as the heat of the sun beat down on them. He spotted a lady of about forty rocking backwards and forwards, muttering under her breath. The whites of her eyes were visible and a cigarette of some kind lay on a rock next to her. Ben zoomed in to catch her expression. In the corner of the shot though he spotted a young girl dressed in a green and red sari. She was not much older than ten, and was in a similar posture. She was rocking back and forth, then suddenly seemed to shake, crying out. Another lady ran over to her as she fell on her back, writhing around. He began to zoom in to capture the moment, but as he did so Rupa put an arm on his shoulder, distractedly pointing at a few ladies further up the hill.

"Let's try and get a few interviews to see what's happening," she said. Ben hesitated, wanting to capture more, then he turned the camera on her as she approached two ladies sitting on a rock. Rupa smiled, asking in Telugu if it was possible to speak with them. They both huddled closer together, pulling their scarves over their heads as they looked nervously at the camera then at each other.

"It's OK," Rupa said soothingly. "We just want to ask some questions about the Jatara. Can I sit?" They looked at each other again, neither responding as they looked at the ground. Rupa took it as an invitation and perched on the boulder as close as possible, without scaring them off.

"Do you live in Agnipatnam?" Rupa asked gently. The women remained seated, but neither offered an answer.

"Have you travelled far?" The younger of the women shuffled her bare feet, still making no move to respond. Looking at their worn saris and cracked hands, Rupa assumed that the ladies were probably both Dalits, possibly from the village and if not, brick workers from a nearby factory. She doubted they would have the finance to have travelled far.

"Have you been to the temple yet?" Almost imperceptibly,

the older of the women inclined her head, still refusing to make eye contact with Rupa. She tentatively pulled back her scarf, revealing a red mark on her forehead with rice clinging to it. Rupa smiled at the progress.

"Were there many Joginis at the temple?" It was the older lady who answered.

"Yes, there are always many Jogini during the Jatara," she said in a hoarse voice, flicking her eyes towards Rupa.

"Have you seen any dedications this year?" The women both looked at each other, wary of how to answer. Rupa waited a moment then rephrased the question. "Were any girls given to the temple?" The older lady looked at her hands for a moment then spoke.

"Yes. There are always dedications. Some are told to give their daughters, others decide to. This is the life of a Jogini."

"Why do they give their daughters?" The woman shrugged.

"Because this is what they do. Their mothers are Jogini, they then become Jogini too. It is the way."

"Can the girls say no?" Rupa enquired.

"Why would they say no? They become part of the goddess. She brings them and their families many blessings."

"But, the girls are then given to the men in the village. Do they not want to take their own husband?" The older woman shrugged, looking at Rupa.

"They need no husband, they are the goddess. This way they bring blessings to the whole village. It is a better life for them. If no-one is dedicated, the goddess will be angry and there will be no rains, then everyone will suffer." The younger woman who was sat next to her nodded fervently.

"Who decides which girls will be dedicated?" Rupa asked. Neither spoke, but Rupa noticed the younger girl flicked her eyes to the older lady in a trance-like state.

"These ladies choose who will be Jogini?" The younger girl wobbled her head slightly to show this was true.

"And sometimes," she began tentatively, "the priest, he will come with the high-caste men from the village. He will choose who will be a Jogini. But sometimes here, they are also chosen by..." she started before the older lady cut her off with a sharp stare.

"Sometimes who chooses?" Rupa asked gently.

"No-one. That is all," the older lady said curtly. "That is the only way it happens." The younger lady sat with her eyes down, feeling abashed.

Rupa decided to change the subject to keep the conversation going.

"Soon it will be the elections, yes? Do you know who you will vote for?" The ladies looked at each other again, defensively pulling the scarves around their faces.

"We will vote for Chief Minister Kalluri and Mr Chaudhury, of course," the older lady said automatically.

"What about the new party? Will you not vote for the Dalit Freedom Party?" Rupa asked. Their eyes widened and they both shook their heads frantically.

"No, we must vote for Chief Minister Kalluri and Mr Chaudhury," they stated again.

"Why *must* you? Surely you have a choice? That is what the elections are for." The older lady stopped for a moment and looked around, being sure to see that no-one was within earshot. She pointed at Ben with the camera. "This, no," she said, wagging a finger. Rupa looked at Ben and lowered her hand to signal for him to stop filming. As she did so, she clicked the record button on her tape player. For the benefit of the tape she asked again, "why do you have no choice about who you vote for?" The older lady leaned in while the younger lady looked about her terrified. She lowered her voice to a whisper, barely audible over the cries ringing out from the crowd at the base of the hill.

"Only yesterday, a Dalit girl was hanged from that tree," she said, pointing to where the events had taken place. Rupa nodded sadly, urging her to continue. "We are not stupid. We know why they did that now. This is to show who has the power, what they will do to us if we cause trouble like she did. We are all scared that if Chief Minster Kalluri or Mr Chaudhury find out we voted against them there will be big trouble."

"Have you ever been in trouble with them before?" Rupa asked. Both ladies looked around before answering. The older lady leaned in conspiratorially, dropping her voice to a whisper that Rupa hoped would still be caught on tape.

"In the past, before he was in power, Mr Kalluri would come to the village before the election and say that if we voted for him, then after the election there would be a new village well and a better school for our children. His men also waited outside the election room and he gave one hundred rupees for everyone who voted for him. Of course we all voted, no-one else would give us this money, but we are still waiting for the school and the well, even though he has promised them to us before *every* election. Last time it all changed though. We were offered no money, but told that if we did not vote for Chief Minister Kalluri and Mr Chaudhury then the whole village would suffer. That night some of the men who had refused to vote for them disappeared." She stopped for a moment, staring into the distance as she recalled the memory. "They walked back into the village late that night, but each of them was missing the finger which they had used to stain the election paper. One or two had lost a whole hand." She stopped again for a moment to regain her composure. "They said that the men who had taken them did not say a word and wore masks, but we all knew who they were. A few of our men died because of the bleeding and the others all found it hard to find work again. Here we work with our hands. If they are injured, there is nothing else we can do. This is why we must vote for them."

"And you are sure that it was Kalluri and Chaudhury who did it?" She nodded, the younger woman placing an arm around her shoulders.

"The men that were taken, one of them was my husband. He only lost a finger, but he was never the same again afterwards. He told me that when they took him, he..." she stopped as a group of six men walked up to them, arms around each other's shoulders as they made up songs in time to the rhythm of the drums as they staggered along. Spotting Ben, they came over, crowding around the camera, each shouting loudly in Telugu for Ben to film them. Ben kept the camera down as he shook his head, trying to wave them away, but they surrounded him, poking the camera and trying to push buttons on it.

"Damn it!" Rupa said, standing up and storming over to tell the men to move on. After a few comments about her needing to dress like a real lady, the men moved off, swaying as they negotiated the slope back into the crowd. When Rupa looked around though, the two ladies had gone and in their place sat the old lady who had rocked back and forth. Her eyes were clear and piercing as she looked at Rupa.

"Yellamma says that you come here to try and bring her harm," the Jogini began.

"I'm not listening to this crap," Rupa said, turning away in frustration. As she tried to turn though, the lady caught her arm, her yellow nails digging into Rupa's wrist. "She says that you are to be warned. It is not safe for you to stay here."

"I bet she says that. What a convenient way to get us to stop filming what is being done in her name. Now excuse me, I have work to do."

"You must stop and leave this place now," she said again, her nails beginning to break the skin on Rupa's arm.

"Let me go," Rupa said, yanking her arm back. The Jogini released her arm and Rupa fell to the ground. As Rupa landed, the Jogini suddenly threw her hands up, grabbing her head as if a bolt of lightning had cracked her skull.

"The fire, the fire!" she screamed. Rupa raised her eyebrows in show of her scepticism. "A fire is coming. You will not survive the fire unless you go now!" the lady screamed, her finger outstretched.

"We'll take our chances," Rupa snorted, turning to go.

Chapter 22

Anitha

Anitha watched as the sun began to drop from the sky, disappearing behind the temple. It had felt the longest day of her life already and she wanted more than anything to go home and see Prabu, to whisper stories in his ear as he slept.

Her head had almost stopped spinning now, but every time it did someone brought her more of the drink that burned her chest and throat. She had learned to stay quiet, hoping they would forget and stop giving it to her. It didn't work though. Renuka, her mother, her aunties, even people she didn't know forced the drink on her until she could swallow no more and it spilled down her front. The ladies surrounding her cackled loudly as they span around in a haze of colours. She wished she could cover her ears and block out their laughter, but it just seemed to get louder and louder, cutting through her.

Anitha was continually poked and harassed; there was constantly another duty to perform. She had prayed, danced, offered sacrifices and eaten holy prashad food which had been offered to the goddess, although all of it had passed in a blur. Her stomach was constantly tense, unsure of what was to come next and how she would deal with it.

As the day wore on, her earlier visions of the fire were forgotten. She saw Renuka safely in the temple offering prashad food to the devotees as they came to make their offerings, everything continuing as normal. She looked and saw the banyan tree towering over the temple, its ancient branches tapping on the roof in the wind. It had been there forever and looked like it would be there for hundreds of years to come. *Just a bad dream* she told herself, passing it off. Maybe it was the drink. It had made her feel strange all day. The dizzy juice was what she had named it in her mind.

Her head throbbed with every beat of the drum and she felt like the drummers had managed to crawl in her ears to bang her head with their sticks. She wanted to scream to try and block out the noise but it vibrated through her entire body.

The sun quickly disappeared, the last of its rays burning out until only darkness was left. She looked at her mother, who stood tall beside her, the flames from under the cooking pots around them dancing on her face, her eyes looking into the distance. As if coming back from a day-dream, her mother shook her head, looked around, and then grabbed Anitha by the top of the arm.

"Come. We must go now," she said anxiously.

"Go where?" Anitha asked wincing, her mother squeezing the flesh on her arm so tightly it hurt. "Can we go home now? Maybe Prabu is better. We can see him?" She didn't know if she had the energy to go one more step, let alone dance or pray again.

"Not yet. It is night time. You have your most important duty to perform now," her mother said as her eyes searched anxiously through the crowd. Anitha felt her stomach turn over as she worried what more she would have to do. She hoped that they would not make her drink the dizzy juice again.

"What must I do Mother?" she asked, her speech slurred. Her tongue felt like it didn't belong to her, as if it was a strange creature in her mouth, doing what it wanted rather than what she told it to do.

"You will see. Someone very special wants to meet you. We must hurry or he will be very angry," she said, weaving through the crowds huddled around their pots, dragging Anitha behind her.

"Who will be?" Anitha called out as she stumbled over a misplaced foot from in the crowd. Her mother yanked her back up to her feet, eyebrows creased in annoyance.

"Come. He will be angry," she said again. The look on her mother's face was one she had not seen many times. She remembered seeing it when her brother first got ill and also when her mother had not been able to pay Mr Harim back the money he had lent her and he had come around shouting and threatening to make Prabu work for him. It was the look of fear. Something had to be bad.

"Must I go mother? Please, can't we just go home? I'm scared," Anitha pleaded, placing a hand on her mother's arm.

"We don't have time for this. He said you must come at sundown. We are already late," her mother said shaking off Anitha's hand.

"But what will I do?" Anitha asked, refusing to move.

"You are Jogini, you must perform your duty," she said, then more quietly to herself she added, "then Prabu will be well." She looked at Anitha again. "Come, we must get there now," she said, pulling Anitha who stumbled after her, submitting to following her mother through the bustling crowd. They passed in front of the temple, the crumbling red paintwork looking as if it was glowing in the lights that beamed from the entrance. Anitha peered over her shoulder to look for Renuka, but she was nowhere to be seen.

The crowd grew less compact as they began to climb the hill on the east side of the village. Up they wound, her mother speeding up as they climbed higher and higher, with Anitha struggling to keep pace. There were no lights up here, and it grew darker the further they went from the cooking pots and lamps held by the crowd. The shadows of the trees scared Anitha, with their branches reaching out in the darkness like long fingers grabbing for her.

Every now and then she would see a figure appear from behind a trunk, looking as if the tree had come to life. They would scramble away, leaving Anitha's heart racing. She didn't know what was real and what wasn't, nothing seemed safe to her.

She felt her way around a trunk, taking care to step over its roots which seemed to move whenever she looked away from them, the constant spinning of her head not helping her to focus. As she passed the roots, fully concentrating on her footing, she almost walked straight into her mother who stood silently between two trees. Her mother looked around, then put her face so close to Anitha's that Anitha could smell the dhal on her breath. The moonlight reflected in her mother's eyes as she took Anitha's head firmly in her hands.

"This is it now. Your first night as a Jogini. You are very blessed. You must do whatever is asked of you, no asking questions like before. There is a very important man who is to take you now, you must go to him, I cannot take you. He is waiting through those trees," she said, nodding beyond Anitha.

"But what is it I am to do? I'm scared, please don't leave me," Anitha said, shaking slightly. Her mother pulled her face even closer.

"You are Yellamma now. She will guide and protect you. You should show no fear. Now, no more questions. You must go straight ahead." She followed her mothers finger, spotting the car headlights which shone dimly in the distance. She could hear low voices and see shadows as people walked in front of the car. Anitha stood watching them for a moment, rooted to the spot.

"Go!" her mother demanded, pushing her forward. Anitha crossed her arms and began to walk slowly towards the lights. She looked straight ahead, counting each pace to give her courage. After she had walked ten steps she turned, looking for reassurance but she couldn't even make out if her mother was still there.

Taking a deep breath, she pushed on, stumbling in the darkness as trunks seemed to leap up at her. Reaching out, she steadied herself with branches which stretched out like arms to support her.

She heard a twig snap behind her and stopped, her heart thumping in her chest. Looking around she couldn't see anyone, and carried on unsteadily until she pushed through into a clearing. Dazzled by the brightness, she stood, shielding her eyes from the glare of the headlights. She could make out at least ten figures standing around, some drinking as they talked loudly, their laughter making her more fearful. She stood for a moment, watching the figures move around as she tried to find the courage to speak. Maybe if they didn't see her she could just go back into the woods. She could go home. Things would be like they had before today. But then Prabu would still be ill. She had to be brave. She was Yellamma now.

Another twig cracked behind her and she turned, hoping it was her mother to say it was all OK and she didn't have to do anything else. In the darkness though, she made out the shape of a big man adjusting his trousers as he walked out from behind the bushes. He strode towards her, his face cloaked in shadow. She heard him chuckle as he approached.

"We've been waiting for you," he said, his face close to hers. "Sir!" he yelled, grabbing the top of Anitha's arm as she yelped. "Your *gift* has arrived. Yellamma has brought you a great blessing."

The men around the car fell silent, and she could sense all their eyes turn to see her trembling silhouette in the car headlights.

"Very good, bring her to me," a deep voice demanded from the middle of the group. The men parted as she was dragged through them, but she could still hear their whispering as she was brought forward as an offering. In her mind she pictured the temple earlier in the day, animal after animal brought there as a sacrifice. She wondered if they had felt as scared as she did now, and if they'd had any more of an idea what was to happen to them.

She was brought forward until they reached a spot not far

from the front of the car, when the man grasping her arm took her by the shoulders to make her stop. Anitha kept her face down, too scared to look up. From the corner of her eye she could see a shadow approaching. She felt it stop in front of her and flinched as a calloused hand gently touched her chin, raising her face towards it. She blinked, trying to adjust her eyes as the shadow began to come into focus. She could see his tired yellow eyes looking at her and she wanted to look away, but he held her firmly so she had to see him.

As his face came into focus, Anitha realised they were eyes she recognised. They were eyes she had seen a thousand times before, although they had never spoken to one another. Her mouth fell open in surprise as she stared at him, trying to understand why he would want her to come here. How did he know who she was?

Everything was quiet as he stood and looked her up and down, inspecting her as she saw the men doing with goats at market. Those that were weak or had a blemish were rejected. Sometimes she would watch in the village square with Javali. Javali would say how much she thought they would sell for, though she was nearly always wrong.

He rubbed a thumb over her soft cheek then nodded.

"A beautiful gift from Yellamma indeed."

Chapter 23

Rupa

Rupa was near breaking-point. She was exhausted and felt completely powerless as she sat on a gnarled tree stump trying to shade herself from the last of the sun's powerful rays. They had rested here too long already, hiding from the pack of men prowling the bottom of the hill in search of her and her news crew. Every time she heard a noise she spun her head around to follow the sound, heart thumping in her chest. She had already seen a snippet of what they were capable of doing, and she wasn't keen to be caught by them again.

If only I hadn't got so involved, she thought. We could have been a long way from here, safe on the road, probably tucked up in a comfy bed in a nice hotel. She sighed. There was no way she should have been so stupid and reckless to allow them to come into this danger. This mess was all her fault. She looked around, scanning the trees, trying to think of a way to get them to safety.

Ben sat on the ground fiddling with the shattered remnants of his camera, still in a rage as he rubbed a finger over the cracked screen. After a few moments he sighed deeply and threw the useless remains to the ground, kicking it away in disgust, then placing his head in his hands. His right eye was swollen shut and was already a deep purple, a sign of their lucky escape.

Stuart sat slumped against a tree for support, his right arm in a makeshift sling crafted from his T-shirt. His eyes were closed and it was hard to tell if he had drifted off or was just trying to block out the pain. His back was covered with red stripes where they had caught him with sticks and his trousers were torn from stumbling on the journey here.

All of them were exhausted, but they had to find the strength from somewhere to keep going. The cover given here by the forest was only thin and Rupa had no idea how many of Chaudhury's bloodhounds were out there. It was only a matter of time before they were sniffed out and torn apart.

There had been six of the brutes earlier but that number had probably increased now they had managed to escape. They hadn't even seen the men coming. They had been trying to film for most of the day, but every time they tried to dive back into the crowd, any useful footage was ruined by drunk men dancing excitedly in front of the camera and trying to shove their whole face on the lens. This had left them frustrated and stranded on the slope, trying to conduct reluctant and altogether fruitless interviews with any villagers who were resting away from the pandemonium. Midway through one of these interviews with an elderly villager, Stuart had suddenly let out a cry as he tumbled to his knees. Turning around, a group of men stood behind him, all dressed in shirts and trousers, wielding bamboo sticks in their hands. The youngest of their party tightly gripped his stick, and swung it down with venom across Stuart's back as he struggled to get get to his feet. Stuart grunted, sprawling flat out on the ground in front of the men. The young man raised his stick again, beads of sweat darting down his neck from the exertion. His eyes bulged and the reddish purple of chewed paan dribbled from the corner of his mouth as he was poised to strike again. An older man stepped forward though, holding his hand up to motion for the young pup to stop. Reluctantly, the younger man lowered his stick, teeth bared as he continued to glare at Stuart.

The older man took another step forward, his heavy frame casting a shadow over Stuart. A white moustache drooped over his top lip and his shirt was stained with sweat. He stood with his legs apart and arms at his side. The other men formed a semicircle facing the news crew with him at the centre.

Ben stepped forward, putting himself between Rupa and the group, camera slung over his shoulder as he raised his fists, eyes darting around nervously. "Come on then, who wants it?" he shouted.

The older man remained calmly standing, raising one hand in the air.

"Come, this is most unnecessary" he said in heavily accented English. "We do not need to be having these unpleasantries. We have come just to be speaking with you."

'Bollocks!" Ben shouted. "That doesn't look like talking to me!" he said, nodding at Stuart who was grimacing with pain as he struggled to get to his feet. Ben held out a hand and helped Stuart to his feet while keeping his eyes trained on the man. "What do you want?"

By now a small crowd was beginning to gather, watching the events with interest. The man held up both hands in an open palm gesture.

"I am sorry for the actions of my colleague," he said, placing a hand on the young man's shoulder. "He was told no to the striking, but he becomes very furious sometimes when people are speaking badly about our Chief Minister Kalluri. The man is like a father to him. Especially when people like you are spreading lies about him."

"We haven't said *anything* about him," Ben said, stepping forward again to shield Stuart behind him, who was wheezing for breath.

The man began to speak in Telugu, directing the comments to the crowd.

"We are not liars!" Rupa shouted in Telugu, stepping next to Ben.

Still with his hands up, the man took a step forward.

"Then please be giving us your camera and equipment. Then we can be seeing what it is you will be saying there."

"We don't have to give you anything," Ben said, tucking the camera behind his back. "You have no right to come up here and try and bully us."

"It is a most sad thing you will not listen to reason," he said, dropping his hands. As quick as lightning, a man to the right of Ben flew at him, catching him with a right hook to the side of the face. Caught off guard, Ben toppled to the floor as two more of the men pounced on him, ripping the camera strap as they hoisted it from his arm.

"Stop!" Ben shouted, "stop!" as he tried desperately to cling onto it. The crowd stood motionless, watching the events with a detached fascination, as if it were a film on a screen. The older man stood, hands folded over his belly with a snarl on his face as the men threw the camera to the ground and stamped on it with their heeled shoes. He shouted to the crowd in Telugu that this was a warning for those who slander the names of their beloved Chief Minster Kalluri and Mr Chaudhury.

Smelling blood, the young pup raised his stick again, striking Stuart across the back of the legs, while another man struck him on the arm. The pain was almost too much for Stuart, as he struggled to hold on to consciousness.

Rupa was grabbed from behind, her arms thrust behind her back as she struggled frantically. In front of her stood one of the men, a rusty machete in his hand. He stared at her with a glassy eyed smile, raising the machete so she could see it. He waved it around as if it was a toy with which he was teasing a dog, then he placed it to her cheek. Rupa held her breath, praying frantically as she felt the steel nipping at her skin. The whole time, she stared him in the eye, not wanting him to see her fear. She would not give him the satisfaction, no matter what he did to her.

After a moment more of teasing she saw the glassy eyed smile droop. Something had caught his attention over her shoulder. He brought his hand to his side, allowing Rupa to breathe once more. She turned her head to see what the commotion was and spotted another group of men marching towards them. The machete-wielder cursed and brought it down, half-heartedly attempting to hide it behind his back, like a naughty child caught eating sweets in class.

"Let them go!" the man at the front of the group demanded in Telugu. He was dressed in a blue pin-striped suit, and was sweating profusely, his hair plastered to his forehead. The men stood still, weapons by their side, but made no move to back away.

"We're here on orders Kuldeep," the fat man replied, arms still folded as he looked sourly at the newcomers.

"So are we. Now let them go," Kuldeep demanded.

"Chaudhury Ji has given us direct instruction to *speak* with our friends here and make sure we reach an agreement, there's no harm in that," the fat man replied, his jaw clenched. "I'm sure Kalluri Sir would see no harm in that either. It is him we are thinking to protect."

"He may not, but Yellamma herself has given direct orders not to harm them."

At this there was a ripple of chatter through the ever-growing crowd. The fat man bristled. He had little time for prophecies and words from Yellamma. 'Religious hocus-pocus' Chaudhury called it, but only in private. He was too smart to declare any such beliefs publicly. Far too many of their supporters gave weight to such superstitions and to speak against it would only alienate them from those who kept him in power.

He could feel the eyes watching him intently for his next move and knew it was foolish to risk a rash action in public. The news crew could wait. The crowd would not always be there to protect them.

"If Yellamma wants them safe, then she can have them," he said, nodding his head to his men, who in turn relinquished their hold on the news crew. He held his hands out in a gesture of goodwill, forcing a smile on his face.

Rupa had managed to follow the whole conversation,

relieved at their rescue, but she was not so naïve to believe this was the end of it. She could see the bemused faces of Stuart and Ben as they were released, baffled by the events going on around them. They looked at her, eyes questioning what was going on. Ben silently mouthed 'Go?' at her and she nodded her head, stepping away from the man who had held her.

Ben bent over, picking up the remains of his camera in a sullen act of defiance as he eyeballed one of the men guilty of its destruction. Stuart remained hunched over, his face screwed up and drained of colour as he looked behind him, his right arm hanging limply at his side.

The fat man continued to speak, his voice projected for the crowd to hear.

"If it is Yellamma's will then who are we to question that?" he said placidly, before leaning in close to Rupa and switching to English. "You best run fast. Yellamma has saved you for now, but we have all of the night to find you." With that he stepped back and held out his hand, gesturing for them to go in peace, a sardonic grin on his face.

Straightening her shoulders, Rupa pulled herself up and marched through the group of men and the crowd that parted to let them pass as they muttered about Yellamma and what the prophecy might mean. One or two touched them out of reverence on the way past, while others fell back. She tried to keep her face taut, not allowing them to see the fear she was feeling, but underneath panic was bubbling up. She didn't look around to check for Ben and Stuart until they were well clear of the crowd that stood like cattle, their eyes unblinking, mouths slightly open. Stuart had his left arm over Ben's shoulder as he hobbled forward, his right arm hanging at an awkward angle.

"What was *that*?" Ben asked as they neared her, his right eye closed as it continued to swell. "Who were those guys that arrived?"

"Let's just say for once we seem to have got lucky. I don't know why, but they seem to think we are to be protected. We'll see how long that lasts. The other group though, they're not just going to let us slink off, we need to find somewhere safe, and quickly. Stuart, are you alright to keep moving?"

Stuart nodded, trying not to let the pain show on his face.

"Looks bad," Rupa said, pointing to his arm. "You think it's a break?"

"Who knows. Let's just get out of here," he said, his face drained of colour.

"So where are we headed then?" Ben asked, looking at her expectantly. Rupa ran her hand through her hair, feeling the burden of responsibility weighing heavily on her once more.

"We can't go back into the crowd, who knows how many others Chaudhury has looking for us," Rupa thought aloud. "We could head back to the van, but they may be watching it." She looked at the wooded area up the hill and shrugged. "This might be our best bet. We'll head down this next valley, and then cut back upon ourselves into the woods once we are out of view. It might buy us a little time until we come up with a better plan." She saw the look of doubt clouding both their faces. "Any better ideas?" she snapped. After a moment they both shook their heads.

A few hours later, they now sat exhausted, licking their wounds while figuring out what to do next. They had been in this copse for at least twenty minutes, making themselves easy targets. Rupa knew she had to get them moving again, especially Stuart who was drifting to sleep by the tree. If he was to lose consciousness now she had no idea what they would do.

"Ben," she whispered. He looked up from his squat on the floor by the broken camera, his right eye now swollen shut. "We've got to get going again. We need to get deeper into the trees. We're sitting ducks here." He nodded and got to his feet, stretching as he did so.

"Any idea on where?" he asked.

"It looks thickest up there," she said, pointing up the slight hill.

"It's going to be tough going for Stuart. He's not in a good way," Ben responded.

"This should at least keep him awake. We need to stop him from losing consciousness."

Suddenly they heard voices shouting to each other less than a hundred yards away. They both froze while Stuart's eyes sprang open, struggling to focus. They waited for a moment, hearts pounding in their chests, not even daring to even breathe.

The shouts came again, this time even closer.

Rupa looked around frantically, then silently pointed to a break in the trees. The boys nodded and Ben strode over to Stuart, rapidly helping him to his feet, and slinging an arm around his waist for support. They heard the shouts even nearer, and hurried quickly for the undergrowth, pushing through the bracken as the dry branches snapped and cracked before them. Every step felt like they were raising an alarm, the woodland conspiring against them to scream out their position.

In their haste, Stuart tripped over a log hidden under foliage sending them both sprawling. They tumbled down a slight hill, rolling through the greenery till they came to a stop at the bottom. Stuart bit hard on his tongue to save himself from screaming out, the pain a blinding light.

Ben was about to leap to his feet when out of the corner of his eye he spotted one of the men about thirty yards away through the trees, his white shirt glowing in the darkness. Ben looked at Stuart placing a finger to his lips, being sure to keep his head down. After what seemed like an eternity the man turned and started walking in the opposite direction, calling out to the others.

Allowing themselves to breathe again they spotted Rupa crouching ten yards from them, her eyes darting around. She motioned with two fingers the direction for them to move in and they proceeded with caution, hunched over as they edged forwards picking their way over fallen tree stumps and overgrown roots. The woods seemed to get denser and denser, helping to cover them as the shouts from behind continued to ring out.

They were in no shape to get far fast though, and within minutes Rupa was aware of a systematic line forming behind them as the men organised themselves, each man calling to the next as they moved forward to see if they could see anything.

Rupa knew it wouldn't be long until they were surrounded. She could hear Ben's raspy breathing next to her, the weight of Stuart dragging him down.

As they pushed on, Rupa suddenly became aware of a dim glow ahead of them, casting shadows through the trees. She could make out dark shapes standing around, hands on hips while others paced back and forth.

Glancing over, she saw Stuart leaning heavily on Ben, his head drooped as he struggled on. The voices behind them were getting louder and clearer but if they continued they would soon be exposed in the light.

"Ben," she hissed, slowing to a walk. "We need to get out of sight. There," she said, pointing a little ahead of them to an uprooted tree stump. It had formed a small cave where the roots had ripped up the earth when it toppled. As quietly as possible they clambered in, pulling foliage over themselves as they became entwined in the dangling roots. They wiped dirt on to their cheeks, hoping to remain camouflaged.

Within a matter of minutes the hoarse shouts began to surround them. Chaudhury's men had slowed to a walk and were talking animatedly among themselves. Rupa could feel her heart pounding and she tried to still her breathing. She prayed for safety, that somehow their flimsy hiding place would not be discovered. In the darkness, she felt a hand reaching onto her arm and almost screamed before she realised it was Ben tentatively seeking her hand. Taking it in his own, he gave it a squeeze for comfort as they sat in tense silence.

Rupa could make out a dark shape moving not more than

ten yards away. From his positioning it looked like he was heading their way. She held her breath as he narrowed the gap to five feet, the acrid smell of his sweat filling the air. He stopped and coughed, staring into the distance, then rested a foot on a root of the tree above them, showering Ben, Stuart and Rupa in dirt and pebbles. They closed their eyes, hoping to remain undetected as he breathed heavily above them.

After a moment one of the other men called out. "They've got to be nearby now. Let's go, they can't have got far."

"What about those lights?" another called out.

"Why would they have lights?"

"It's Kalluri. Has to be," shouted another to their left.

"They might have made it to him. He'll be keeping them safe."

"I say we tell him to hand them over," one shouted back.

"They might not have made it that far, let's keep looking," another called.

"It's too dark. We'll never find them here."

"We have to find them. What will the boss say?"

"What will the boss say if we get old Kalluri all riled up?"

"Who cares?"

"Our fight is not with Kalluri, it's with those dirty Dalit dogs. We need him. He is on *our* side."

"If he's on our side then why don't you go and ask him to hand them over?"

"Why don't you?"

"Are you scared of him?"

"No. I'll go in there now and tell him to give them over now, filthy reporters."

"Let's cut them. We'll make him give them over."

The man in front of their tree stump spat and they heard it land a yard or so away. "Nobody is going in to speak to Kalluri." Rupa recognised the voice as the fat man from earlier. His voice cut through the fighting with authority. "We head back and see what the boss says."

"But they could be just here! We can't go already," someone demanded.

"Let's look a bit longer."

"We head back *now!*" the fat man said again, his voice firm, challenging anyone to resist.

A tense silence fell, the atmosphere charged while the men stood shuffling their feet. After a moment Rupa heard footsteps as one of the men turned and began to walk back through the woods. One by one the other men stalked after him, some complaining in hushed tones. Rupa let out a low breath, suddenly aware she hadn't breathed through the whole altercation. She relaxed her sweaty hand in Ben's and they parted their grip in the darkness.

After waiting to be sure they had all gone Ben propped himself up on an elbow. "What happened there?" he asked, completely bewildered.

"It seems we have Kalluri to thank for keeping us safe again," she said, gesturing with her head towards the soft glow of the headlights.

"I think I could actually kiss him!" Ben said, and they all laughed nervously. Their muted conversation instantly fell silent again though as they heard a nearby branch crack. Rupa's heart fell. It had all been a ruse to get them out of hiding, and in their relief they had fallen for it.

They waited, the next footstep taking a moment to fall. Tentative footsteps, gently brushing the dry ground, not the heavy stomps they had heard before. The sound of bells softly chimed with each advance. They were approaching, reluctantly picking their way through the undergrowth. The three of them waited, listening to see if other feet joined them, but they remained solitary. Rupa shared a puzzled look with Ben, then dared to lift her head ever so slightly and peer into the darkness, spotting a slight female figure approaching, hugging herself tightly as she edged forward.

As she got closer, she passed right by where they were hiding and Rupa was able to make out that she was only young, maybe no more than twelve, and dressed in her finery. The girl kept pausing, unsure on her feet as if she was drunk. She stumbled near them, steadying herself on one of the branches that shielded their den. She was within touching distance of them, but seemed oblivious to anything around her, focused only on the distance. She pushed on, like a moth heading towards the lights, and they all popped their heads over the base of the tree, watching her halting progress.

"That's weird. I wonder where she's heading?" Ben asked. Rupa responded, her thoughts tumbling out as she pieced together what they meant. "She's headed for the lights. Kalluri is at the lights. She's going to them, but why now? Unless.... she must be a Jogini! The Jogini is going to Kalluri."

They both turned to look at her.

"You mean…?" Ben asked, struggling for the words. Rupa nodded solemnly.

"First night. She is going to be given to him." An awkward silence fell as they continued to watch her timid steps towards the light, the chime of bells growing fainter with each step. What if it was Anitha? Rupa thought to herself. She had promised Mansa to try and protect her if she could, and now Anitha may have literally crossed their path. She had to do something. Just before she spoke, Stuart cleared his throat.

"As long as Ben helps me, we can do this," he said in response to the question they were all mulling over. Surprised, they both looked up at him.

"I'm OK," he said, looking ahead, his eyes pained as he watched the girl.

"You're not OK, look at yourself man," Ben said, "who knows what you've done. You're in agony."

"We've been threatened, beaten and had to run for miles in this bloody wood! If we can't at least *try* to help here, then what good has it all done?"

"Dude, there is nothing we can do. Even if we get your busted ass all the way over there, what will we do? We're not exactly going to be able to fight them all, and if you hadn't noticed back there our camera isn't exactly in mint condition to do any filming."

"True," he said, reaching into his pocket, letting out a gasp of pain as he did so. "But, for this, I reckon my little friend might do the trick," he said, pulling out his iPhone. "It's not exactly HD but it lets us catch what's happening. The zoom is pretty decent, so we don't have to get much closer."

"I like it mate, but there's still no way you can creep over there. They will hear you from a mile away and we're not leaving you here alone. Pretty sure we have used up all of our lives for today."

"Ben's right, Stuart. You can't go any further and we can't leave you here alone. I'll go by myself."

"No chance. You can't claim it's too unsafe to leave me here alone then you go off by yourself! You know what they will do to you if they catch you filming this!" Stuart hissed.

"I'll only go close enough so that I can catch it on camera. If we see him taking her off in the car then at least we've got something. I'm not going far."

"But…" Stuart began, before Rupa reached out, placing a hand on his phone.

"I'll be ok. Back in five minutes. You make sure you keep yourselves safe."

She turned to go and Ben reached out, grabbing her wrist. "Just…well, be careful yeah?" he said. She bit her lip and nodded, turning and following after the girl in the dark.

Chapter 24

Mansa

Mansa suppressed a sly smile. It had worked, although she had no idea how. She pulled the shawl over her head and turned away, hoping to avoid detection and questioning as she pushed out of the crowd that had gathered to see the altercation. She hoped Rupa and her team would be safe. She had done all that she could to help, but she had to go now if she was to get to the meeting place for Anitha.

Luckily Kuldeep had always been pious. When Mansa had served at the temple he would visit at least every few weeks, always seeking her or one of the other Joginis for prophecies. Ever since Mansa had correctly guessed his child would be a boy, he had hung on their words hoping for more blessings. She knew that he would listen to her even if she was despised by some of the other men in his group. She had managed to catch him on his way back to Kalluri and as she spouted off about the news crew being a blessing sent from Yellamma, he drank in every word she said. She could read the scepticism in the eyes of some of his men, but no-one would speak out against Yellamma, especially not without Kuldeep's approval.

Things had worked even better than she could have hoped. He had stormed straight towards the crew on the hill, ready to offer them protection. Curiosity had won out against her better judgement, and she had followed after him to see how it would work out. So far their arrival had halted the violence that was beginning to escalate against the news crew.

Pleased to have played her part, Mansa took the opportunity to slip away, fearful she may face questioning if she remained. As she walked off she could hear Kuldeep's tone of authority silencing the dissenters.

She only wished it was as simple to help Anitha. All she could do now was get back to the banyan tree and pray that somehow Anitha would manage to break free and come to her.

She thought back to her own dedication many years ago. By this stage in the day she was already inebriated, stumbling backwards and forwards, unsure of what she was doing and terrified at the lack of control she felt. It would be the same for Anitha now. Would she even be able to find her way to the tree in that state? Should she go and try and find her instead? The decisions were too difficult and the outcomes too important to leave to chance. If only Anna Ma'am was here to guide her. She would know what to do.

Mansa paused for a moment, trying to clear her head amid the madness around her. Maybe she would see Anitha on the way, she thought. She could figure out something then. She had to get to her before the evening. She couldn't bear the thought of what they would do to her tonight. Images from her first night flashed across her eyes and it took all the strength she could muster to push them back to the dark place from where they had arisen.

Mansa pressed on, her eyes desperately scanning the crowd for a glimpse of her beloved Anitha.

Chapter 25

Rupa

Rupa scampered forward through the foliage, trying to keep the girl in sight without allowing herself to be seen. In her hurry she stepped forward, the crack of a dry twig underfoot causing the girl to pause and look around, before continuing unsteadily on her way. She was like a new-born deer picking her way along.

As the light from the car got brighter, so too grew the volume of voices of the men gathered in its glow. She was close enough now to understand snippets of their conversations as they stood with bottles of lager in hand.

She watched the girl as she left the shelter of the trees, nervously standing on the edge of the clearing as the men continued chatting, oblivious to her presence. The sight of the child standing there, hugging herself innocently before she was thrown into this filthy adult world was too much for her. Rupa could film all she wanted, expose the perpetrators, but she would never be able to take back what they were going to do to her. The girl's innocence could never be returned. Rupa had to get to her before she was discovered.

Rupa moved out from the foliage, remaining low to avoid drawing attention as she stalked forward, keeping her eyes on the girl and willing her to stay rooted to where she was. As Rupa moved though, heavy footsteps crunched to her left. Without hesitating, she threw herself down into the bracken, and lay still, sure that she had been seen. The steps moved closer to her, until she heard them stop a few feet away. She swallowed, her throat dry as she waited for what was to come.

She heard a belch, and then flinched as an empty beer bottle struck her on the leg. It took all she had not to call out. A man began whistling, and it became clear to Rupa that he had not seen her. This thought was confirmed as a second later she heard the zip on his trousers, then saw his urine spraying off the dry twigs. She could hear it landing just inches from her, but remained still, muscles tense as she screwed up her nose.

It seemed like an eternity before he finished and zipped up his trousers, and she could hear his whistling moving away from her. She rolled over and watched him lurching away through the woods, as he took a moment to lean against a tree and light up a cigarette. For a brief moment he seemed to have fallen asleep, before he straightened up and dragged on the cigarette, the bead glowing bright in the darkness. He paused for a second, his gaze moving from the floor, around the woods, before resting on the girl.

The girl still stood oblivious to his presence as she watched the men wandering around before the car headlights, silhouettes casting fear into her heart. For a long moment she looked back over her shoulder, as if ready to disappear back into the woods. Rupa focused the camera phone on her, zooming in to capture the fear on her face, as she willed her to turn and run. Watching through the camera, Rupa saw her turn at the sound of the man's cough as he jogged over to her, grabbing her roughly by the arm. She looked terrified as he smiled at her, yanking her forwards to make her move. She stumbled into the clearing, the other men turning as he called out to them.

"Damn it!" Rupa cursed under her breath, as she crawled through the foliage after them. She kept the camera phone on them, the girl putting up little resistance as she was pulled forwards like a small rag doll. Rupa stopped as she reached the spot where the girl had stood seconds earlier. Crouching, she held out the camera, recording all of the commotion. A drunken cheer went up from the crowd as the men all gathered to see the girl being brought before them. Without instruction they formed into two columns, the girl paraded down the centre of them as the men leered, lustful smiles on their drunken faces.

At the front an older man stood and waited for her to arrive. She was handed over, like a bride being brought to her husband in some twisted ceremony. Rupa zoomed in as close as she could, the girl completely frozen as the older man pushed a strand of her hair behind her ear, whispering something to her as he did so. Anitha gasped as she recognised the silver haired man who had been made of flames. It was hard to guess what was said as the girl offered no reaction, her face immobilised with fear.

As Rupa saw the man, she realised their suspicions had been confirmed. Their research from yesterday had thrown up picture after picture of the most powerful man in the state, Chief Minister Kalluri. He looked much older than even the most recent pictures suggested, many creases lining his tired face. Yet despite that, even from a distance, there was an air of authority about him. At a single word, the rowdy crowd were hushed, each looking to him for instruction. His voice boomed out into the night.

"Tonight gentlemen, is a night for celebration. I have received a great blessing from Yellamma which I intend to enjoy!" The men roared with laughter. "So for now, I suggest that you go and enjoy yourselves too. Go!" he said, waving his arms to disperse them. Some of the men raised bottles in the air as others turned, putting their arms around each other's shoulders and wandering out of the clearing and into the woods to Rupa's right. Luckily, none came near enough to worry her, so she continued filming Kalluri as he talked with two of his men, pointing to the car and then smiling as he patted them on the back.

Within a few minutes the whole clearing was empty, apart from the two men Kalluri had spoken with who stood guard on either side of the car. Rupa could hear the shouts and laughter of the others disappearing through the woods as they headed back to the village.

Left alone, Kalluri put a hand on the girl's shoulders and ushered her into the back of the car, looking around the woods one last time before he joined her and pulled the door closed behind him.

Rupa pressed the stop button as a hot tear coursed down her cheek.

Chapter 26

Anitha

Anitha heard the car door click shut behind her. She scuttled along the seat to the far side, pushing herself against the other door. The handle dug into her back as she pressed against it, trying to make herself as small as possible. Her heart was beating at a million miles an hour as she stared at the man. Chief Minister Kalluri, that was his name. Something about him frightened her. Maybe it was the way people did what he said straight away. It could have been the fear of why he had brought her here to this car alone. Or maybe it was the strange way he was looking at her now.

After Javali had been hanged everybody said that it was on Kalluri's orders. She wondered if he going to hang her too. She hadn't been speaking with any boys though, especially not any from a higher caste. Maybe someone saw her in the field with Javali when she had met the boy. She wanted to tell him that she hadn't done anything, but she felt too scared. Kalluri sat down at the other end of the seat, slumping in the chair as he undid his top button and sighed deeply.

It was the first time Anitha had been in a car, and it was much bigger than she had imagined. It was nearly the size of her hut. The chairs were so soft and comfortable it was like sitting in a big pile of long grass.

Despite the heat outside, it was cold in here. She could feel the small hairs on her arm rising up and a shiver ran down her back. She hugged herself to dispel the cold and feel a bit safer.

Anitha's eyes darted around as she tried to see if there was a way she could escape. Mr Kalluri chuckled from in the corner and she looked back at him. He had both arms behind his head and his legs stretched out in front of him.

"You don't have to try and run away, I'm not going to hurt you girl." Anitha continued to stare at him, wide-eyed, as she pressed against the door, both feet now up on the seat as she curled into a ball.

He sighed again, then stretched his arms above his head causing the joints to crack. He stared at her for a moment, looking from her anklets up to her face. A slight smile touched the side of his mouth. Reaching out he rubbed some sequins of her sari between his chubby fingers. She watched him, terrified.

"You like the presents I sent for you?" he said, flicking one of the anklets so that it chimed. Anitha pulled her leg back in horror. Why had he got her these? What did he want from her?

"Come, sit here," he said, patting the seat next to him. For a minute she remained where she was, not saying a word. She chewed on her bottom lip, wondering what she should do. "Come," he said again, this time more firmly, and she knew she had to do as he asked. It was the same tone her mother used when Anitha was in trouble; one which you couldn't argue against. She slowly uncurled and sat on the seat, tucking her sari under her and then resting her hands on her knees. She sat rigidly, trying to keep as large a distance as possible from him.

"I have another present for you," he said, reaching over and pulling two slender glasses from under the chair in front of him. He handed her one and then pulled a dark green bottle from a small box in front of them. He ripped the golden wrapper from the top and threw it to the floor. With a grunt of exertion he pulled the cork from the top and bubbles spilled everywhere as it made a loud popping sound, making Anitha jump.

"You like champagne?" he asked. Anitha had never heard the word and just continued to stare blankly at him. "Of course you don't. What Dalit has tried champagne?" he said, answering his own question. He took the bottle and poured some into her glass, his hand shaking slightly as the bubbles spilled down the side of the glass and onto her sari. "Damn shakes! Can't seem to stop them," he said, as he poured a glass for himself. He drank it down in one, then smacked his lips together loudly. Anitha sat there, glass in hand, still staring at him. "Well, drink then!" he ordered, tipping the bottom of her glass with his finger. She wondered if it would be the same as the drink earlier that had burned her chest. It didn't smell the same though. It smelled sweet. Timidly she took a sip and coughed as the bubbles went up her nose. He smiled slightly as he poured himself another glass. "Feeding good champagne to dogs. What would Chaudhury say, eh?" he mused, more to himself than her. She hoped it wasn't to her as she had no idea what he meant.

"You don't talk much, do you girl?" he asked, as he knocked back his second drink. Anitha shrugged.

"Have you got a name?" he asked. She nodded.

"Well? What is it?"

"Anitha," she said, looking down at her sari where the

bubbles had soaked in. It had been so pretty at the start of the day, but was now torn and covered in marks from all the spilled drinks. She wondered if he would be angry that she had ruined his gift to her.

Kalluri nodded and poured himself a third glass. This one he drank more slowly, allowing the bubbles to dance on his tongue as he sat deep in thought.

"You're scared of me, aren't you?" he asked after a long silence. Anitha was unsure of the correct answer, so she just sat and looked at her lap.

"Of course you are. It's alright, you don't have to be frightened. I've told you before." He paused again for a moment. "Chaudhury used to fear me too. There was a time when he actually did what I said. Not any more though. Only yesterday, he had that girl hanged. That wasn't my idea. Chaudhury did that one, right behind my back." Anitha could see how tightly he was squeezing the glass, and was scared it was going to break. He looked into the distance as he spoke, more to himself than Anitha. "That wasn't the first thing he did behind my back either. He's getting out of control, like a train with no driver. There are limits in politics. You have to do things right. Take it slowly. He won't listen though. This is how the young are, think they know it all." He pulled out a fat cigar and felt below his seat for a sharp knife a few inches long, the golden handle decorated with a large cat, it's eyes some kind of green jewel. Very carefully he used the knife to trim the end of the cigar, and then tried to place it back in the box under his seat, but dropped it as his hand shook again. "Damn it!" he said, placing the cigar in his mouth, puffing as it lit, the thick smoke quickly filling the back of the car.

Even through the smoke Anitha could see that he was tired. His eyes were red and puffy and his face seemed like it was folding in on itself. She could feel the sadness clouding his voice.

"I have raised him as a son for all these years. Given him position and power, but he still wants more. He will never be satisfied." He drew a long puff on the cigar and blew the smoke over his head as he closed his eyes. "You can't make enemies everywhere. You have to be shrewd." He stopped and looked at Anitha, taking her in. "Look at your people. This Dalit Freedom Party, they are getting more and more support while ours diminishes. Joining with them could be the only way for me to stay in power. It's not going to happen with Chaudhury fighting everyone else. This is a new era. People's views are changing. This new state of Telengana is causing all sorts of problems, headache after headache. His fighting and squabbling definitely isn't helping our cause. Every time I manage to sort out one riot, he manages to cause another." He finished the champagne in a long gulp and then chuckled to himself. "But what do you care, eh? You are only a girl. Here I am talking about politics when there are far more interesting things that we can be doing."

He pressed a button to make the window go down, and threw out his cigar, before putting his empty glass on the floor and turning on his elbow to face her. "Yellamma has given me a beautiful blessing in you. A reward for all my hard work and devotion," he said, lifting one of his hands and clumsily brushing the hair from her face. Anitha shuddered slightly, involuntarily drawing her face away. In that moment his tired eyes seemed to change, suddenly coming alive and dancing with fire. He put a hand on her leg and Anitha pulled away, frightened.

"I've told you, I won't hurt you," he said, putting a hand behind her neck, and leaning forward he pulled her head towards him, kissing her hard on the lips. His stubble was sharp against her face and she could taste the smoke from his cigar. She tried to cry out, but he pulled her mouth against his. After what seemed like forever, he let go and she wiped a hand across her mouth, looking at him in horror. Anitha couldn't find any words to say, but shook her head as she looked at him pleadingly and backed away into the corner once more.

"Come here girl," he said, "you don't want to make me angry." She remembered what her mother had said before. She had to please him to make sure Prabu would be OK. She closed her eyes and breathed deeply, hoping whatever would happen would be over quickly. When she opened her eyes, she could see that he was beginning to take off his belt, a tight smile on his lips as he looked at her. She sat there, held in the corner by fear despite her need to obey and save Prabu.

"I said, come here, *now!*" he said, his voice rising as he pulled the belt free from his trousers and threw it to the floor. Anitha closed her eyes, and pulled up her knees to her chest, scared of what was to come.

At that moment there was a click as the car door opened. She looked over to see a slim figure climbing in from the darkness. Startled, Kalluri rolled over, cursing as he did so. "Chaudhury? What the hell do you think you're doing?" he asked, as the man sat himself down next to him, dusting off his shirt with his hands as he did so. "Can you not see that I am busy?" Kalluri said, motioning with his head to Anitha.

"This won't take a minute. Then you can get back to your...*business*," he said, looking at Anitha with disgust.

"This had better be good," Kalluri said, straightening up in the seat and buttoning the top of his trousers. "Especially after that stunt you pulled yesterday with the hanging. Have you any idea what damage that has caused?"

Chaudhury shrugged. "Someone had to do something. A Dalit girl running around with a high caste boy. Polluting our villages, sending out a message that it was fine, and yet, once again you failed to do *anything* about it. *That's* what is causing damage! You make us look weak. The filthy dogs are running wild in the streets, doing whatever they want, and you let them. You are letting this state go to rot. Then you let this news crew brazenly walk in and film it all, making up whatever lies they want to about us."

"If you didn't give them cause to film, they would have had no reason to come here. You brought them here with your antics and then you want me to clear up your mess?"

"I am more than capable of looking after myself," Chaudhury continued. "It is you who does not even raise a finger to warn them, allowing them to do what they want. It is just the same as you treat those Dalits. I bet you would have just left the girl alone after what she did. You are too busy trying to keep everyone happy."

"You know the danger that the Dalit Freedom Party are to us. You have seen the riots in other villages, yet you deliberately infuriate them, doing it all in *my* name! How is that going to help us? You have gone too far this time."

"If I have gone too far it is only to make up for *you* not going far enough. They are the enemy. These lower castes who must be crushed, and yet you sit here, making a fool of yourself with a Dalit girl to get blessings from Yellamma. Look at yourself! Everyone is laughing at you. You've become a joke." At that, Kalluri leapt over and grabbed the younger man by the throat. Even though he was older, he was much heavier, trapping Chaudhury under his weight.

"I'm a joke?" Kalluri said, increasing the pressure on Chaudhury's throat. "I'm a joke? You have destroyed any relationships we have built in these communities. Any votes we may have got, you continue to undermine with your arrogance and violence. Even the higher caste voters are turning away from us, they don't know what you will do next. You have become a whirlwind of destruction. Do you know what your own party call you? '*The tsunami*' because you destroy everything you touch. No more. We are done!" he said, releasing Chaudhury, and sinking back into his seat, breathing deeply from the exertion. Chaudhury sat for a moment, rubbing his neck as his eyes blazed with fury.

"We are done? What will you do without me? You wouldn't be where you are without my support. You are nothing without me! I'm the one who got us where we are today. Me!" he said, beating his chest. "You're the one who is going to throw it all away. You can't make it without me. Alone, you are nothing!"

"Oh yes I can," Kalluri said smugly. "After your stupidity yesterday, I spoke with Rani." Chaudhury sat bolt upright at the mention of the leader of the Dalit Freedom Party.

"Rani? But, he...he's our enemy," he said slowly, trying to make sense of what he was being told.

"Sometimes an enemy's enemy becomes a friend. He has got all the lower caste votes already. If I join with him we can bring in votes from the high *and* the low castes, whereas you just lose me the votes I had already won. Even if we split to Telengana, we can reach an agreement on some Dalit seats on the council to keep people happy. You're finished Chaudhury! Now, get out of my car!" Kalluri demanded, pointing to the door.

"What? How could you? You would leave me for some filthy Dalit mutt? You make me sick! I will never forget this. Never!" he said, jabbing his finger into Kalluri's chest.

"Just shut up and get out," Kalluri said, swatting Chaudhury's hand away then slumping into the seat. "I don't want to see your face ever again!"

Before Anitha knew what was happening, Chaudhury had picked up Kalluri's belt from the floor and had it wrapped around its owners neck, tugging it as tightly as he could. Kalluri's arms flailed around wildly, while a horrible gurgling sound came out of his throat. Anitha screamed, trying to press herself as far away from it all as she could.

Kalluri managed to kick Chaudhury, causing Chaudhury to slip, but in his fury he leapt straight back onto Kalluri, putting his knees by his throat as he tugged the belt. Kalluri snarled like a bear as Chaudhury pushed a hand in his face in an effort to be free, using his weight to tip Chaudhury off him. Panting heavily, he whipped the belt from his neck, throwing it to the front of the car. Chaudhury looked around in panic, spotting the knife which had been discarded on the floor. Picking it up, he threw himself at Kalluri, driving it into his chest. A heavy gasp escaped Kalluri as the white seats were covered with crimson. Chaudhury drew the knife out again, and crazed he drove the knife into Kalluri time and time again until his limp body slumped to the floor, weeping blood from the numerous stab wounds. Chaudhury knelt on the seat, panting heavily as he looked at the body before him, his own shirt and face plastered red. He dropped the knife, before wiping his trembling hands on his trousers. A bloody bubble rose and burst on Kalluri's lips as Chaudhury sat and watched his chest rise and fall for the final time.

Chaudhury sat transfixed, until a whimper from Anitha reminded him of her presence. She sat with her feet drawn up on the seat, trying to avoid the puddle of blood collecting on the floor, her eyes trained on Chaudhury.

He looked at her and bared his teeth, like a wild animal ready to attack its prey. Anitha grabbed at the door handle, desperately fumbling with it while the seat bounced as Chaudhury sprang for her.

He tried to grab her neck with one hand, but slipped on the bloodied leather seat and managed only to get hold of her thaali necklace and a handful of her hair. He tugged at the necklace, the thread biting into her neck before it snapped, spilling the shells all over the back of the car. Before he could rise, she finally pushed open the door and tumbled out from the car into the heat of the night. Rolling over she saw Chaudhury scrambling to get to his feet. Frantically looking around she spotted two men a short distance away, listening to dance songs on their mobile phones as they drank beer and played cards by the moonlight.

Emerging from the car, Chaudhury screamed out "Chief Minister Kalluri has been killed! The girl, she did it! Stop her, quick!" The men looked over at the commotion, then jumped to their feet, knocking over a number of beer bottles as they did so.

As they gave chase, Anitha turned and ran towards the woods, not daring to look back around as she heard the cries for her to stop.

Chapter 27

Rupa

Rupa jumped into the hole right next to where Ben was sitting, kicking up a cloud of dust as she landed.

"Wow! Don't scare me like that!" he said, trying to keep his voice to a whisper. "You ok?" he asked as she wheezed for breath. She held up the phone as her response and passed it to him.

"It was Kalluri," she said between breaths. "I got him. Recorded. He took her. Into the car."

"Great work," Ben said, nodding solemnly as he turned the phone to watch it. Rupa put a hand over the screen.

"There's no time. We can't just leave her. It's not right." She caught her breath. "Ben, we have to try and stop it. There are only a few men there with him. He sent the rest off."

"Rupa, look at Stuart," he said, pointing to where Stuart was curled up and sleeping among the twigs just a few yards away, his eyes roaming as his body twitched. "I can't just leave him. It was me who talked him into this in the first place."

"But she was so near. I should have stopped her before she got closer to them," Rupa said, holding out a hand in the darkness as if she could still stop it. Ben could hear the anguish in her voice.

"There was nothing more you could do. Look," he said, holding up the phone. "You got that creep on camera. You need to think of the big picture. This is going to destroy him. That was our aim wasn't it? Catch the bigwigs playing dirty and take them down. It's going to stop lots more occasions like this."

"She's not an occasion. She's a girl," Rupa reminded him, her voice flat. Ben sighed.

"You know I didn't mean it like that. We have to be sensible though. Stuart needs to get to a hospital and what exactly would we do when we got there?"

"I don't know, *something*. Anything is better than the guilt of doing nothing." They sat in silence for a moment, pondering her words.

"I can't leave Stuart," Ben eventually reasoned. "He's got to be our first priority."

They heard a rustle next to them, then Stuart's voice, thick and slightly slurred, from among the leaves. "Go! I'll be just here. If they were coming back for us they would have done it by now. I don't plan on disappearing anywhere."

Rupa looked at Ben expectantly. He pulled off his cap, ran a hand through his hair then put the cap back on. "Alright. We'll go check it out, see what's what. If it looks in any way dangerous we are coming straight back. Understand?" She nodded.

"Come on then" he said, "sooner we get there, sooner we get back."

Rupa knew that something had happened long before they reached the clearing. The eerie quiet she had expected was broken by angry reproaches shouted between the men. As they drew closer, she saw that numerous people had returned to the clearing. They were pacing frantically back and forth, many hollering into mobile phones or talking animatedly with each other.

"I thought there was only a few of them?" Ben said.

"Something must have happened."

"Like what?" Ben asked. Rupa shrugged, crouching low to avoid detection and motioning for Ben to do the same.

They cautiously approached to see what had stirred the men up. Rupa managed to catch snippets of their exchanges, trying to piece together the different conversations. As they got nearer, Ben leaned in and whispered in her ear. "What are they saying? What's happening?"

"It's Kalluri," she said. "Sounds like something has happened to him." As they reached a viewpoint of the clearing, all their questions were answered. In the car headlights, the body of Kalluri was laid flat on its back, his arms and legs spread wide as his head lolled to the side. His shirt was soaked in blood, and the grass glistened where his body must have been dragged to the light, a snail-trail of red leading from the car. Two men were kneeling next to his lifeless body, one wailing as the other shook his head in silence, consumed by grief. The others charged around aimlessly, all barking instructions at the men as to what they should do next with no-one taking notice. A few ran off in varying directions, searching through undergrowth, but on the whole confusion reigned.

Ben and Rupa looked at each other stunned.

"What?" Ben silently mouthed to her. She shrugged in confusion, trying to assemble the scraps she could pick up in the pandemonium in to some kind of logical order.

"Can't be far…." one cried out.

"This means war. We'll make the Dalit dogs pay!" another shouted, pumping his fist.

"Found the shells from her necklace all over the body," one commented.

"Be looking out for that bitch. She must have used some *powers*," one near them was saying into his phone.

"The girl. She strangled him with his belt then stabbed him to death. We must find her," two men were saying as they walked nearby.

"Apparently she had a whole gang of them working with her, filthy Dalits!"

"I saw them," another said. "Whole group of Dalits attacking the car, singing as they did it!"

She turned to Ben, perplexed. "Apparently it was the girl!" she whispered as she grabbed his arm. "They are saying she strangled him with his belt then stabbed him."

"What!" he exclaimed. "No way! How could someone that small kill him? She was tiny and he was a pretty big bloke," Ben said, holding his arms out to denote the size of Kalluri's stomach. Rupa shrugged, her eyebrows deeply furrowed.

"That's what they're saying. Some claim she had a group of men with her. Maybe he was too drunk and passed out? These guys seem to have been drinking all day. Who knows what strength you find when you're forced to fight for your life? They're saying her necklace was all over the body, maybe he grabbed it when she was strangling him?"

"That doesn't prove a thing!" he said. "There's no way she could have done that, not that they are likely to care if they can prove it or not. What have they done with her?"

"They haven't found her yet. No-one seems to know where she's gone. They're all shouting at each other to go and look for her, but no-one seems to be moving. Guess they're missing their leader."

Just then someone walked by within about ten yards of them. They held their breath as he stalked past shouting orders for someone to check over the other side of the clearing.

"We need to get out of here," Rupa whispered. "Whatever happens next there is going to be a lot of trouble."

Chapter 28

Anitha

Anitha knew the men would not stop chasing her. She had once seen a pack of wild dogs come into the village following an injured monkey. They had hounded the monkey until they managed to corner it. Gnashing and growling they'd ripped it apart and killed it. It was one of the most horrible things Anitha had ever seen. The dogs were chased off by some men from the village with large sticks, but she remembered the determination the dogs had shown as they hunted it down.

They were hunting her now. As she ran they were probably shouting for her to stop, but all noise was drowned out by the sound of blood pounding in her ears. Too scared to look back, she continued into the darkness hoping that she could somehow manage to lose them as the trees grew thicker. She ran quickly, but had no shoes and had to fight from screaming out as the sticks and thorns cut into her feet and branches grabbed at her sari.

One thing kept her tired legs moving as she stumbled through the trees: home. If she could just get back to her mother then somehow everything would be OK. She could explain what had happened and her mother would tell them it wasn't her fault. Then Anitha could tell her mother she didn't want to be a Jogini anymore. Things could get back to how they were. She could look after Prabu and help in the house and not have to visit old men in their cold cars.

The woods were empty as Anitha ran and after a while she dared to stop and catch her breath. Leaning against a tree, she peered behind her, but could no longer see the men who had been giving chase. She bent over gasping for breath then felt her stomach tightening before she began to vomit onto the dry ground. The back of her throat burned. As she finished she wiped her mouth with her hand. She shivered and could feel tears welling up in her eyes.

As she leaned against the tree for a moment's rest, she heard gruff voices farther away in the woods shouting and asking each other if they had seen her. It was not time to stop. Rest would have to wait until she reached home.

She continued picking her way through the trees, trying to still her breathing and move away from where the voices were. She could hear them gradually getting quieter as they moved to another part of the forest. Hitching up the bottom of her sari she began to run again, hoping to put as big a distance as possible between her and the men. She had no idea where she was heading, the trees all looked the same in the pale moonlight. They grew thicker, then thinned out, then grew thicker again. She was unsure whether she was still moving away from what had happened, or was just heading back to the car, but knew she had to keep moving. She couldn't stay still.

Exhausted, she eventually tripped over a rock, and landed in a stream that was winding through the woodland. She knelt in it for a moment feeling it flowing over her aching legs. She cupped the cool water and tipped some over her head before greedily scooping it into her mouth. She dipped her head under, the coolness of the water beautiful against the heat of her skin. The river wasn't very deep, when she put an arm in, it only came up to her elbow, but at the side were many rocks which looked like they were probably covered by the floods during monsoon season.

Looking around she realised she had been here before. There was a large tree on one side with an old bit of tattered orange rope hanging down from one of its branches. Javali had brought her here a few times and they had swung on the rope, with Javali daring her to jump off. She had been too scared though. It had taken all her courage just to grab onto the rope in the first place. Javali had told her that during the monsoon they would come back and jump from the swing into the river. They never had though. Now they never would.

She stood and walked out of the water, her wet clothes weighing her down. Touching the tattered rope gently with one hand she said a silent prayer for her lost friend and thought about the conversation in the car where Mr Kalluri had blamed Mr Chaudhury for Javali's death. Even if it was true, it didn't change anything. She still would never get to see her friend again and play together on the rope swing.

She sighed. There was no time to think about these things. She had to keep going before they caught up with her. There were probably more men looking now. At least she knew where she was. All she had to do was follow the stream and it would lead her back to the watering-hole in the centre of the Dalit wada. From there it was only a few minutes back home.

Anitha walked most of the way in the stream, the cool water soothing her sore feet. As she got closer to home she could hear the gentle rumble of the crowd in the distance, the celebrations of the Jatara continuing long into the night. The sound was somehow comforting after the eerie silence of the woods. She looked up to see the occasional explosion of fireworks in the sky; red, white and orange filling the darkness and guiding her home as a small 'pop' rang out, followed by a dull cheer. Every year she would stand and watch them, Prabu laughing as she gasped at the sound.

She soon came out from the trees, the stream trickling into the watering hole in front of her. Looking around nervously she came out into the open from the covering the trees had provided. She could see no-one one near the woods, but she feared what the shadows were hiding.

On the other side of the water she saw people dancing, arms around each other as the drum beat on. She could make out the temple and the small fires that still illuminated it. Her mind flashed back to her vision from earlier, the temple dancing with flames, but she shook her head. It must have just been bad dreams from the dizzy juice they made her drink.

Looking left then right she took her chance, gathering up her wet sari and running as fast as she could all the way back around the watering hole, down the stony path and straight to their small hut. She paused briefly at the entrance, the whole place dark and silent. Maybe her mother was still out, she thought, but she would usually leave a small candle burning for Prabu.

Prabu was always left some light while he slept. When

they had been younger, Anitha had been scared of the dark. At night she was certain shadows would come to life, walking around the room trying to find her. She had told her mother but she had only laughed and told her not to be a coward. She was no longer a baby so she shouldn't act like one. There was nothing in the darkness to fear. Prabu had heard them talking though and the next day he had told Mother it was actually him who was scared of the dark. He asked if he could have a candle lit every night to give a small bit of light, promising to work for longer in the cotton fields so that they were able to afford it. Their mother reluctantly agreed and Prabu had made sure there was always a small candle burning at night until Anitha was asleep. She remembered the first night they had lain on the floor to sleep with the candle between them, its dull glow lighting Prabu's features. She had smiled at him and he had given her a wink before rolling over to sleep.

Anitha entered timidly into the darkness, the air feeling too thick to breathe. A strange smell lingered in the air, a smell that reminded her of decaying fruit at market. Over the distant roll of the drum she could hear quiet sobs coming from the darkness. It took a moment for her eyes to adjust.

"Mother?" she asked timidly. "Is that you?" The sobbing stopped and she saw a dark figure slowly uncurl and move towards her. As it got closer she could make out the soft edges of her mother's face.

"So, you have come back," her mother said in voice that didn't sound like her at all. Anitha wanted to know what was happening, why her mother was upset, but the emotion of the last few hours was too much and bubbled out of her before she could stop it.

"Mother, it was horrible. I was taken into the back of his car and then..." she began, but stopped as her mother slapped her hard across the face, drawing blood from Anitha's lip as she did so. Anitha drew back in surprise, placing her hands on her face.

"Don't call me 'mother' anymore," she said. "No daughter of mine could be so selfish. You have taken away all that I have. You are cursed!" her mother screamed, her voice becoming hysterical as she shook Anitha by the shoulders. Did her mother already know about what had happened in the car? Was she being blamed for what had been done?

"I don't understand. What have I done?" Anitha asked, scared and confused.

"Did I not tell you that you are a Jogini? You have duties to fulfil. Why then are you back here?" she asked, holding Anitha firmly by the shoulders as she shouted.

"Because they took me into the back of the car, and then horrible things happened. The man..."

"You were to stay there. You cannot come running back here before you have fulfilled your second pattam."

"But it was terrible."

"Because of you, because you cared more about yourself than us, you have brought ruin on this family. I explained what your duties are and yet you ran from them. And now, because of your selfishness, your brother is *dead*!" she said, and with that let out an agonising wail, clutching her stomach as she huddled over and wept.

"No!" Anitha screamed. "He can't. Today he was getting better. It must be a mistake. I went and did everything asked of me. He must be ok," she said, trying to place a comforting arm on her mother's shoulders. Her mother threw off Anitha's arm in fury.

"Get away from me! I never wanted you and now you have taken everything away from me. Get out. Get out! *Get out*!" she screamed, her arms flailing as she chased Anitha from their hut.

Arms over her head, Anitha tried to protest but it was in vain. Her mother chased her to the path outside their house, picking up the clay jug of water and hurling it at Anitha's head, which flew just over her shoulder. Anitha turned to face her and her mother raised a quivering finger.

"I never want to see you again. You are no daughter of mine." With that she spat on the ground and turned back inside the house, huddled over, embracing herself as she wept bitterly.

Anitha stood rooted to the spot as she watched her mother disappear back into the darkness of their hut. For a moment she considered going after her, but there was nothing she would be able to say.

She couldn't believe that Prabu was gone. There had to be a mistake. Was it her fault? Was she the one who had done this to her brother? They had all told her that if she fulfilled her duties he would be well again, even the priest and Renuka. Was this a punishment from Yellamma because she had not served her correctly? She had drunk all they gave her, she had danced, said the prayers and performed the trances. She must have done something wrong though because it hadn't worked. Maybe if she went back and did things properly she could bring her brother back? But now, that was impossible. Not after what had happened. If she was to try and go back they would hurt her like they had Javali. The bad man, Mr Chaudhury, had shouted to the men that it was her who had hurt Mr Kalluri. He was a liar, but who would listen to her instead of him?

Maybe she deserved to be taken and hanged from the tree for what she had done to her brother. Maybe if it wasn't for her, he would still be here now.

Full of remorse, she staggered down the road and sat weeping in a patch of tall grass until she felt there were no more tears inside her. "I'm sorry Prabu," she whispered over and over as she rocked herself backwards and forwards, all the while watching the hut as if by some miracle her tears would bring him back to life and he would come walking out, tossing an old cricket ball or chasing the chickens down the road.

Suddenly, from the corner of her eye she saw some commotion. A number of men, all dressed in shirts and trousers began running out of the woods and charging towards her house. She recognised a few of the men as those who had been by the car earlier. The one at the front boasted a large moustache, and gestured in front of him towards their hut before charging straight in.

Anitha gasped as she watched another three or four men follow him, all stooping to fit in her hut. They had found her home. There was nowhere she could go now. There would still be other men in the woods and no relatives would take her in after what she had done to Prabu. The temple wouldn't offer any refuge. Maybe if she went over to the men and explained everything they would be kinder? She could say what she had seen, but that would probably get her in even more trouble. Chaudhury was their leader.

She could hear the men shouting and knew it wouldn't be long before her mother told them that she had been there. She couldn't stay here. Thinking about where to go, a sudden thought surfaced in her mind. She had to find Mansa Auntie by the banyan tree. Maybe *she* would still want to see her.

Wiping her tears with her sari, she reached down and unclipped her anklets letting them fall into the grass. Nothing good had happened since she put them on, and she would be quieter without them. She looked once more at the hut and began to run again, this time towards the banyan tree and as far away as she could get from home.

Chapter 29

Mansa

Mansa had forced her way from one side of the crowd to the other, the temple serving as a beacon to guide her amid the sea of animated revellers. As she picked her way through the fires and blood-soaked ground she saw a troop of young Joginis lining the front of the temple, some sipping on alcohol while others muttered prayers, their eyes vacant. They were all surrounded by numerous devotees, eagerly seeking blessings.

Mansa desperately scanned every young face as she passed, hoping to find Anitha, but as suspected she was nowhere to be seen. Peering into the darkness, the light from the fires played tricks on her as figures appeared then vanished. She pushed through the girls, some tutting, others oblivious to her presence as she desperately chased shadows. In the flickering light her heart caught on occasion as she thought she had glimpsed Anitha, but it was never her; always another girl with the yellow stripes of the Jogini on her head and cowry shells around her neck.

After walking the length of the temple walls, Mansa resigned herself to the fact that Anitha could not be found within the packed crowd. She could search for days and still not find her. It was too vast. She must be patient and wait, hoping that Anitha would be able to find her by the banyan tree.

The tree stood to the east of the temple, ancient and proud. Onwards she marched, pulling her shawl tightly around her face as she entered the area full of Dalits. She had grown up among many of them and did not want to be seen now. There were too many questions and unfriendly faces.

Glancing around she checked that Anitha was not already there, but despite the crowds, the area at the base of the tree remained empty except for a few children playing in its huge roots. In the flickering of the fires she could make out the opening to the cavern within its roots, and she headed towards it, trying to avoid drawing attention to herself.

Suddenly a bony hand wrapped around her wrist. She looked down to see the wrinkled face of her old neighbour Venkataramana peering at her through her thick glasses. They were held together with a small piece of wire that looked dangerously close to gouging out one of her milky eyes. Her lips drooped over her gums and as her mouth opened it reminded Mansa of the dank cavern of the banyan tree.

"Balamma?" she asked, using Mansa's arm as leverage to pull her closer. Her glasses rose up and down as she tried to focus by opening and closing her eyes.

"No. I am not Balamma. Let me go," Mansa responded, trying to pull away. The woman's grip tightened though as she began to smile.

"Yes. Yes. You have returned. Yellamma has called you back to us. You are a Jogini again?" she slurred, spit dribbling down her chin as she rolled a shell from the necklace between her fingers. As she turned away to alert the others, Mansa tried to get free, tugging her arm from the vice-like grip. The sudden jolt wrenched Venkataramana from her feet causing her to bump into a number of men. Interrupted by disturbance, the men turned to see what was happening. One pointed at Mansa and began shouting excitedly to the men standing next to him. She felt another hand grab her other arm near the top in a tight grip, a body pressing against hers as she smelt cheap alcohol being breathed into her ear.

"We've missed you Balamma," someone said from behind her.

She shook to get free, but was held too tightly. The men began to press in, shouting drunkenly at her as she closed her eyes and turned her face away. She could feel them towering above her, as their hands pulled at her, causing her to feel faint in the oppressive crush. She was about to fall, the heat and smell almost overwhelming her, when an almighty screech cut through the crowd. It seemed to go straight through her head, slicing it in two. The arms behind her disappeared, doubtless being raised to his ears to block out the noise, causing her to stumble backwards. She landed on her back, looking up to see everyone around her wincing as they tried to stop the sound.

As the noise stopped, people began shouting angrily. Her head was left with a tingling as she waggled a finger in her ear to try and return her hearing to normal. Looking around she saw hands stretched out, pointing at the temple, people nudging each other to make sure everyone was watching. Animated conversations broke out as people craned their necks to see what was happening.

Maybe this was the moment for Chief Minister Kalluri's big speech that everyone had been waiting for? It was rumoured that it was going to bring big change, although whether for better or worse she didn't know. She suspected whatever was said was likely to cause some sort of trouble. Politics here always did. Whatever was happening, she had no interest. She wanted to distance herself from it as much as possible.

Dusting herself off she rose to her feet, backing away from the distracted crowd while the opportunity arose. She broke free of the squeeze of bodies, and was nearly by the tree when a voice stopped her in her tracks.

"Listen to me! Listen to me all of you!" Silence fell across the whole crowd. It was the first time since before sunrise that there had been a moment's quiet, the incessant drums finally hushed. Immediately she recognised the voice as Chaudhury's, trembling with emotion. The whole crowd jostled to get a better view of what was happening. Mansa paused. She needed to go while the opportunity was there, but she had to see what was happening. There was something about the urgency in his voice. This wasn't just a political speech. Maybe it was something to do with her actions earlier. She hoped nothing had happened to Rupa and the news crew.

She stood on tiptoes, peering over the multitude of heads before her, just able to make out the figure of Chaudhury charging up the steps of the temple, two at a time. Usually immaculate, his white shirt was untucked and covered with what looked like blood, as were his trousers. His silver hair was swept all over the place, some flopping over his eyes as he swept it away with his free hand, the other gripping the microphone. Even from here she could make out that he was trembling slightly, his gestures wild as he turned to address the confused crowd, some covering their mouths in shock at the state of him.

"Chief Minister Kalluri is *dead*!" he screamed. As one, the crowd gasped in shock, some shaking their heads, while others cried out. Chaudhury raised his hands for silence as thousands of voices clambered to express their disbelief. "I was with him just now. I tried to save him," he said, voice cracking as he motioned to the blood on his shirt. He took a moment to compose himself. "I saw it all happen. There was a whole gang of them, ten, maybe more. They were laughing as they did it, saying they were in charge now. They said that they will stop at nothing until *they* have the power." Mansa exhaled deeply, bracing herself for what she knew was to come next. He raised a bloodied finger and jabbed it towards the fields beyond the back of the temple. Mansa felt as if it was directed solely at her, despite the multitude of people.

"It was those dirty Dalit dogs!" he screamed at the top of his voice, enunciating every word. "We must not stand for this!" He said, pumping a fist into his palm.

At that, the whole place seemed to explode. Neighbours turned on each other, shouting and screaming as fists were raised. She saw flaming torches being thrown within the compressed crowd as it swayed and surged, pushing forwards then backwards. At the edge of the crowd Mansa turned to run, heading for the protection of the banyan tree. Terrified screams were going up from all around as she clambered over one root, then another. Debris seemed to be raining down from the sky as people raised arms over their heads to protect themselves. A large stone struck her on the foot as she neared the cavern. She cried out in pain, but hobbled on, not even stopping to see the damage as she lowered her legs into the cavern. Dangling them below her she sought a firm ledge to put them on as she held her weight on her arms. In the dark she felt one, the stone strangely cool on her feet. Adjusting her weight onto her good foot, she took one last look at the pandemonium around her. People were scrambling up the tree's roots while others ripped branches from the trunk, waving them around for protection as the crowd pressed in on them all. She hoped that she would be safe tucked away under the roots.

Just as she was about to duck into the cavern she heard a crack above her that sounded like thunder. Looking up she saw a man tumbling, closely followed by a large twisted branch that cracked her on the skull. After that, all she saw was darkness as she slipped into the cavern.

Chapter 30

Anitha and Mansa

It was him. Even with his ripped clothes and tangled hair, Anitha would have recognised him anywhere. As he held up his hands a silence fell and everyone stopped to listen. Her heart was thumping in her chest. All she could picture was the crazed look on his face as he had sat on Chief Minister Kalluri's chest, stabbing the knife into him again and again as the Chief Minister cried out from under him. The groan as Mr Kalluri's final breath had escaped. Then Mr Chaudhury's hand, reaching for her. Stretching out as she tried to get free. Pulling at her necklace. His hands closing around her throat this time. She shook her head, trying to get rid of the thought.

He stood there now, microphone in his hand as he shouted at the crowd for quiet. What was he going to do? He had tried to say it was *her* who had killed the Chief Minister as she fled the car. Was he going to do that now? Would he tell everyone here that she had done this horrible thing? His eyes swept across the whole crowd and she was sure that he was looking straight at her as he began to speak.

"Chief Minister Kalluri is dead!" he screamed. Anitha's stomach lurched. She was trapped in the centre of the crowd with no escape. If he was to point at her and say that she did it everyone would believe him. She was just a Dalit. She would be torn apart in seconds, just as the monkey had been by the wild dogs. Or maybe they would do the same to her as they had to Javali? She was sure she could feel the people around already looking at her, ready for the order from Mr Chaudhury.

His next words surprised her though. As she braced herself to be publicly exposed he spoke instead of a group of Dalits who had come and committed the crime. Confused, she stood with her mouth open as the crowd around her cried out in disbelief, beginning to push and shove those around them. "Filthy Dalits!" someone next to her shouted. "We must stop them!" another shouted, trying to push through to the side of the temple where most of the Dalits were gathered.

"No! No!" she yelled, waving her arms. "It was him! *Chaudhury* did it! It was *him* who did it, not any Dalits!" However, her voice was drowned out amid all the other cries as everyone fought to make their outrage known.

She was pushed in the back as the crowd surged forward, chaos breaking loose. A man in front of her bent down, picking up a rock and launching it as far as he could. Others began to do the same, throwing things in protest with no concern as to where they landed. She was pushed this way and then the other, surrounded by angry faces and hurtful words.

Terrified, she tried to keep her feet amid the shoving. All around her, arms were raised, pointing fingers and trying to protect themselves from the debris being thrown. Anitha was caught on the side of the head by a stray elbow, making her head buzz. Putting a hand to her head she ducked down, trying to stay below the forest of arms above her which offered some protection from the flying debris. Slowly she began to creep forward, hoping to escape the crush and make it to the banyan tree. If she could just make it there, maybe she would be safe.

She could hide in the roots with her auntie until all of this trouble passed.

In front of her a man fell, struck by a flaming stick. The torch landed on the ground, its flames leaping up at ladies' saris, but luckily not catching fire. Somebody picked the torch up, hurling it back into the crowd from where it had arrived, yelling furiously as he did so.

She saw a man near them dressed in a white top and lunghi being thrown to the ground by a group of men. "Dalit!" They screamed. "Murdering Dalits! You will not hurt us!" The men began to kick and punch him, the man's screams lost in the pandemonium around them. No-one came to his aid as he called for them to stop.

Anitha wanted to scream that she had been there and seen it all, but it was impossible. By now Mr Chaudhury was probably a long way from here, driving home in his ice-cold car. He had been the one who had hurt her friend Javali too. It wasn't right that he should get away with it all. How many more people would he hurt?

Furious at how unfair it all was she pushed on, edging along with her arms out to keep her balance. After a while she peered through the endless sea of arms to see how far she had been swept along. The temple was much nearer than before, but she yelped as she saw the banyan tree. She was only a short way from it, but several of the branches were ablaze, torches nestled in the higher reaches. There were also a few people around the base, many waving torches or tossing them into the dry, gnarled roots. The blaze seemed to be spreading rapidly.

It was near the tree that the fighting was the most intense. The Dalit population had all congregated there during the Jatara and were now surrounded, the upper castes raining down kicks and punches on men, women and children. Many fled, but the crowd was too tightly packed to allow an easy flight path. It was a becoming a bloody massacre.

As the tree began to light, the crowd started to disperse, falling back towards the temple. Anitha spotted her opportunity and pressed on, picking her way through the crowd that was now moving back. As she neared the tree, she could feel the heat of the blaze warming her face. On one side, the roots were now flaming, thick plumes of smoke billowing up into the sky. She moved forward while people pushed against her, hurrying away from the blaze. A few branches lay on the ground, already blackened from the flames.

If her auntie was here, surely she would have run with the rest of them, Anitha thought. However, her auntie's her last words lingered in Anitha's mind. "I will wait in the cave until you come. I will wait forever if I have to." Anitha had no family left. She was all alone. Perhaps her auntie was still by the tree, waiting for Anitha to come? She desperately looked around the crowd, but could not see her anywhere. She had to check, just in case...

Anitha coughed as the smoke tickled her throat, so she pulled her scarf around her face to try and block it out. Darting forward, she ran around the base of the tree until she spotted the cavern, the firelight illuminating the entrance. It was still untouched by flames, but the blaze was quickly spreading, dancing along the spiny roots towards the trunk. She looked around at the bystanders to see if her auntie was among them, but nearly all that remained were groups of men waving their sticks triumphantly in the air.

Among them she saw a lady facing away who looked like her auntie. Anitha pushed forward for a better view, but as she watched, the lady bent over and hoisted a small child onto her back, revealing her face as she turned to run away from the fire. Anitha kept looking, scouring the numerous people lying on the ground, some crying out, others silent. She crouched down, looking at those who resembled her auntie in any way, but she was nowhere to be seen.

Of course she wasn't. Anitha had let the whole family down. Prabu's face appeared before her, his face cold and clammy, eyes closed. Her own brother, the one she loved most in the world. She could have saved him but she didn't. Why would anyone be here for her after that? Especially her auntie who had turned her back on the family years ago. Anitha's mother had told her that her auntie had thought she was better than everyone else in the village. She said that she was too good for life here. Surely now she would think that she was too good for Anitha as well.

She cast one last glance back at the tree, clueless about what to do next, when she spotted a lady half out of the cavern, arms laid out over her head as she lay still on the ground. She was tucked into one of the roots, nearly hidden away from view. However, as the flames jumped, Anitha was able to make out the cloak her auntie had been wearing earlier, as well as the bandage wrapped around her head, which was now almost black with dirt. Anitha sprinted forward, leaping over the people who lay strewn on the ground and past the fallen branches, some already reduced to piles of ash as fresh flames rained down from the sky.

Kneeling down she saw that her auntie's hair was matted with blood as she lay with her face pressed into the dirt.

"Auntie!" she shouted, shaking her by the shoulder. "Auntie!" she screamed, but there was no response. "Auntie, come on! Let's go!" she said, getting her auntie's arm and pulling it, trying to drag her free from the cavern, but Mansa wouldn't budge at all. "Auntie!" she shouted over and over, putting her hands around Mansa's shoulders and trying to pull her from the cavern. Over and over she tried, but it was impossible. She yanked hard but ended up falling over, fear rising as she desperately looked around for a way to get her auntie free.

The whole time Anitha could feel the heat growing stronger and stronger, the skin on her face beginning to tighten. The smoke hurt her eyes, and she had to stop to cough after every unsuccessful attempt. She jumped as a branch fell a few feet from them, ricocheting off of the trunk and rolling onto the withered grass.

"Come on Auntie. We have to go now!" she yelled, looking around for a way to get her to safety, but there was nothing to be done. "*Please*! We have to get you to safety."

One more try, Anitha told herself. Bending down she locked her arms around her auntie's chest. Bending her knees, she pressed one leg against a root, trying to get leverage. Her auntie groaned as Anitha heaved, her body moving slightly, ribs now fully out of the cavern. A bead of sweat rolled down

Anitha's face and stung her eye as she strained. She pulled as hard as she could. She could feel her auntie moving. A little more and she would be there. The tendons in Anitha's neck bulged as she put every ounce of effort in to the lift. Her auntie moved a tiny bit more, then stopped, her body a dead weight in Anitha's tired arms. Anitha bent low, then pulled hard once more but failed to move her auntie at all this time. Exhausted, Anitha finally collapsed to the ground panting for breath.

It was no use. Her auntie was stuck and the fire was quickly closing in on them. What more could she do? Anitha felt tears of desperation coming as she gasped for breath. She had not managed to save Prabu and now she had failed to save her auntie too. She was useless.

Cradling Mansa's head in her lap, Anitha gently brushed some of her auntie's matted hair from her lifeless face. Anitha leant over and kissed her gently on the temple.

"I'm so sorry. It's all my fault" she said sadly as she took her auntie's hand in her own and waited for the fire to consume them.

Chapter 31

Rupa, Mansa and Anitha

Despite the shouting and screaming that surrounded them, Ben had managed to capture Chaudhury's speech on his camera phone. He held it slyly so as to not draw attention, but he needn't have worried. For once nobody was giving them the slightest bit of notice; all eyes were fixed on Chaudhury as they listened to his rant, completely mesmerised.

"He's saying it was the Dalits. That's not going to go down well. Quick, follow me, *now!*" Rupa whispered frantically in his ear just as the place went wild. She grabbed Ben by the wrist, pulling him along behind her as he in turn supported Stuart, trying to form a barrier of protection to shield Stuart's injured arm.

"Did you get it?" she called over her shoulder.

"Yeah, decent shots too for a camera phone even if I do say so myself," he said, trying to hold the three of them together as the torrent of the crowd sought to destroy everything within it. The crowd was so tightly-packed though that they were barely moving, apart from the occasional surge one way or the other as someone toppled over, getting lost under the stampede of feet.

"Keep filming," she said, letting go of his wrist. "If we can capture this along with the girl being taken into the car, we just might be able to cobble something together." He decided caution was no longer necessary, extending his arm to swoop a panoramic shot of what was going on. It was sheer chaos, the camera catching debris being tossed and pixelated torches hurtling through the air.

"OK, that's enough. We have to get out of here," Rupa said, her eyes scanning around for possible escape routes. "Stuart, how are you doing?" she shouted. He weakly held up a thumb and forced a smile before grabbing Ben for support again as the crowd tried pulling him backwards.

It was complete madness. There was no way they could survive for long with the fury of the crowd being unleashed all around them. They had to head for the van. It was the only place that would be moderately safe right now. She pushed on, shouldering through the crowd as the boys followed, anxiously looking around to avoid any flying objects.

After a few minutes she felt a tug on her arm and looked around to see Ben squeezing her around the wrist to get her attention. He was gesturing to near the temple.

"Everyone seems to be heading over there. Can you see that massive tree? It's burning up!" She looked and spotted the ancient banyan tree succumbing to the flames. "People are jumping out of it and everything. I have to try and catch it on camera, we can show the hysteria he's caused or something." The crowd was pulling them in that direction anyway. Maybe it would be easier to follow the flow; the van was past the tree. She nodded her consent, and they allowed themselves to be dragged forward.

As they got nearer though they noticed that the tide appeared to have turned. People were now pushing back, fighting to get away from the blaze as it glowed like a furnace, the heat intensifying as it consumed more and more. Rupa tripped and Ben caught her forearm, helping her keep her balance. Looking down she saw a badly beaten man outstretched by her feet, his face flat against the ground. She could see that there were casualties everywhere, sprawled out in the middle of the riot. As people pushed against them, little notice was given to the human blockades covering their path and they were trampled underfoot.

Ben had the phone out and was capturing every detail, looking down to the bodies, then up to the blaze. Swooping to the right he managed to spot a branch falling from the tree and landing in the middle of the temple roof, the tiles smashing and spraying to the ground.

"Have you got it? Ben, we really have to go!" Rupa was shouting as she tugged at his arm.

"Just a sec," he said, scanning along to the tree, and filming the blaze which was quickly covering the tree like a monster trying to devour it. He zoomed in to show its ferocity when he spotted a shadow moving amongst the swirls of orange and reds. It was grabbing at something, trying to haul it free of the roots. Letting it focus he could make out a young girl, scarf around her face as she tugged at the arms of an older lady. The older lady was like a cactus, half above the ground while the rest was buried below.

"Come on Ben, let's go!" Rupa demanded again, pulling at his arm.

"Hang on. Look!" he said, filming the girl continuing her fight to pull the older lady free. She glanced, and then grabbed the phone from Ben. Despite the smoke, she could clearly make out the girl. Rupa had stood and stared at the back of her green and red sari wishing to stop her, and now here she was. She had been given a second chance to help her.

"It's her isn't it?" Ben said, the determination on his face plain to read.

Rupa nodded. "I have to help her. I owe her that much."

"But look at the flames! I can feel my eyebrows tingling from here! There's no way you can get any closer." Without responding she turned and ran, becoming a shadow to Ben and Stuart in the smoke.

"Damn it!" Ben said. He looked at Stuart, "Can you…" he began, but Stuart dismissed him with the back of his hand.

"Go. But be quick man, you've not got long," he said, motioning to a branch falling near the shadows in the haze. He nodded and sprinted away, leaving Stuart alone to watch the blaze, praying for their survival.

As Rupa got nearer, she saw the girl fall and land on the ground, not even attempting to get back to her feet. She leaned over toward the lady, then sat, unmoving, as the flames danced closer. By the time Rupa reached them, the smoke was so thick that she could no longer see them but had to call out, guided by a terrified small voice. Groping around, she felt a small arm and grabbed on to it.

"Are you OK?" Rupa said in Telugu, crouching as she did so.

"Auntie," the girl sobbed. "Auntie, Auntie."

"It's alright, we can help your auntie," Rupa said, feeling around until she touched the lady's shoulders and locked hands around her waist which was buried in some kind of hole.

"Rupa!" a voice cried out frantically from among the smoke. "Rupa!"

"Here!" she shouted. "Hurry Ben!" He raced in, almost toppling over them in the darkness. He touched her back, then felt around for the older lady, instructing Rupa to get one arm while he took the other. Heaving, they felt her shift slightly but something was trapping her from moving any further.

"Something's stopping her. Hold on!" Ben shouted as he blindly felt the ridge she was doubled over with his foot. He stepped down into the cavern, and released her legs from a branch they had become tangled in, before swinging them to the ground above. He then scrambled back up from in the cavern.

"She's out, but we're going to have to drag her," Ben said, his eyes streaming with water as the smoke stung them. Hoisting her up, they each managed to place an arm around her back, letting her legs dangle limply below.

"You OK?" he shouted to Rupa. She nodded then realised the gesture wouldn't be seen.

"Yep. Let's just get going quickly." They began staggering forward, struggling with the extra weight. As they walked, Rupa called out to soothe the girl and to let her know where they were. The girl remained silent, but Rupa could feel her fragile fingers reaching out and grabbing her top for reassurance in the darkness.

The heat was almost overwhelming and they could see an orange glow behind them where the trunk by which they had been standing was now catching fire. Disorientated, they had to keep the glow behind them, the only way to be sure they were heading in the right direction.

Rupa remembered a documentary she had watched as a child where an explorer had fallen from a canoe and got sucked into a whirlpool. As he was pulled under he tried to swim for the surface. In his confusion though he was actually swimming down, and the more he panicked the faster he swam away from safety.

She hoped they were going the right way now. They had to be, but what if there were flames in front of the tree too? The swimmer had been sure he was right, but the faster he swam the further he got from the surface. Arms flailing, his thrashing legs only served to drive him further from safety. In his panic his chest tightened, oxygen running out. Yet he kept swimming. Deeper. Deeper. Down into the murky depths.

Rupa stumbled, her head spinning. The lady fell too, almost on top of her, but somehow Ben kept her from the ground. She couldn't see anything but she felt Ben by her side shaking her. She just wanted to sleep though. A long sleep. To dream of green fields and sunshine. A boat. She was rocking on a boat. Clear skies. She could hear the birds squawking over her head. The boat gently rocking.

Rupa began to cough, her throat so dry it felt like the act of swallowing was ripping the inside of her throat. She was out of the cocoon of smoke, on her back, able to see the night sky above her. Her body tingled as she drew in air. She tried to sit but was too dizzy. Stuart's worried face appeared above her.

"You OK?" he asked, eyebrows knitted together, his

forehead creased.

"Yes," she rasped through dry lips. She tried to lick them, but her tongue was like sandpaper.

"Do you think that you can move?" he asked. She gently nodded her head, then realised why Stuart was the one asking the questions.

"Ben?" she asked. "Where's Ben? Did they all make it out?"

"He, he's going to be fine," Stuart stuttered, glancing nervously over his shoulder.

"Where are they?" Rupa asked, ignoring the dizziness as she pushed herself on to her elbows and looked around. The earlier crowd had rapidly dispersed and they were stuck in what looked like the aftermath of some of the battles she had filmed in Somalia. Bodies lay strewn around them, some unconscious, others groaning in pain. Much of the ground was soaked in blood, although if it was human or from the earlier animal sacrifices, she could not tell.

The bodies were like debris left after the ocean of the crowd had gone out. The temple was completely empty, now just a blackened shell as flames danced from among the ruins. In front of them was a thick wall of smoke rolling closer and closer.

Stuart flicked his eyes towards the smoke to show her where they were.

"No! They can't be! We have to go and get them!" she said trying to push herself up, but Stuart placed a firm hand on her shoulder.

"We'll never find them. Where would we begin?" he

asked, the black cloud consuming all in its path. "Ben said to make sure I kept you safe."

"But it's not fair. It's my fault they are there. I have to help," she said, before doubling over and coughing, yellow dots dancing before her eyes.

"We have to get back, this smoke is going to keep spreading," Stuart said, struggling to keep his tone neutral.

"But if I just get in there, I can shout and..." she began.

"I said *move*! We both know that won't make the slightest bit of difference then we will be lost as well as them," Stuart shouted, frustrated at Rupa for her decisions, the fear of losing his friend bubbling over. She looked up at him, her eyebrows raised in shock. Meekly, she stood and began to back away as quickly as she could, the whole time her eyes scanning the smoke, hoping to detect some kind of movement.

Every time a wave of smoke billowed she expected to see them emerging, but it was never more than an illusion, her mind tricking her. Stuart stood silently next to her, trying to peer through the smog. After a few moments, he turned away, his head lowered.

"It's no use. They can't have survived in that." Shoulders slumped, he sighed and stared at the remains of the crowd still fighting a safe distance from all the flames. Running his left hand through his hair he felt tears biting his eyes.

"Wait!" Rupa yelped, "There, *there*!" she pointed to movement in the smoke. A moment later three figures emerged, black and hunched over, but slowly edging forward. Ben was holding the lady over his shoulder as the girl gripped tightly to his arm. Coming out of the smoke, they staggered about twenty metres before Ben collapsed to his knees, the others going down with him.

As he fell, Rupa and Stuart hurried to them. Rupa took his face in her hands, almost unrecognisable under the soot that covered everything. His skin was dry and cracked, his cap missing and his hair singed. He looked up at her with bright-red eyes that struggled to focus. He opened and closed his mouth like a fish, his throat too dry to speak. Rupa put a finger over his lips to stop him from trying.

"You did it! You saved them!" She whispered in disbelief, before coughing violently. He just stared at her, dazed, not comprehending what he was told.

"Black. Everywhere..." he rasped, his eyes roaming around wildly.

"It's OK, you're safe now. We have to go a bit further though. Then we can rest." Even though they were free from the cloud, the air was still poisonous, every breath burning deep in their chests. Rupa coughed into her sleeve, the force of it shaking her whole body. She felt a hand on her arm and looked down to see the girl at her side. It was impossible to tell that her sari, now black and filthy, had been new and fresh at the start of the day.

The girl was shaking, the hand on Rupa's arm serving to keep her steady. "Thank you," she said in Telugu. Rupa put an arm around her shoulder as they both looked down at the older lady. She was lying flat out on her back, but was now gently moaning, her eyelids flickering as she began to regain consciousness.

"Mansa," Rupa said, bending over and caressing the hair

from her face. Rupa then looked up at the girl standing by her shoulder who was anxiously staring. "You must be Anitha." The girl's eyes widened and she nodded her head.

"You did it. You saved your auntie!"

Chapter 32

Mansa, Anitha and Rupa

She wasn't dead. The intense pain in her head was proof of that. Any slight movement sent a sharp jolt through her skull. She breathed quickly in short sharps burst, her chest feeling like someone was scratching it with their nails.

She remembered getting ready to climb into the cave and wait for Anitha, but everything after that was blank. How much time had passed since then? What had become of Anitha? She could be anywhere now. The thought broke her heart in two. Anitha was gone. Mansa knew she had failed her. Maybe this pain was her punishment for that. Despite everything, she had not managed to protect her. Hot tears ran from the corner of her eyes at the realisation. It would have been better if the fire had just taken her, rather than sparing her for this pain.

Her eyes felt thick and heavy as she tried to open them but she succeeded in squinting to stare at the ceiling above her. It was familiar, but she couldn't quite understand why. Suddenly, a blurred head appeared above her. As it came in to focus she knew that she recognised the small timid face staring down at her. It was the face of an angel. The face of her beloved Anitha. Was she dead after all? She blinked, waiting for the vision to pass, but it remained. Anitha's troubled face came into focus, her eyebrows creased as she leaned over. There were streaks through the dirt where it was possible to see that she had been crying, but apart from that her face was thick with soot.

A small trembling hand reached out and touched Mansa on the cheek then pulled away. Anitha bit her lip nervously then gave a small smile. If Mansa had felt the touch, then it must be real.

"You're alive?" Mansa asked in amazement through her cracked lips. Anitha nodded. The relief was almost too much for her. She closed her eyes and gave thanks, tears pouring down her face. Reaching up she touched Anitha's hand with her own, squeezing it to make sure it definitely wasn't a dream. "I thought, when the fire came, I didn't...." Mansa stammered. Anitha just nodded. "I know auntie," she said. They stayed there for a moment in silence, the joy an anaesthetic to Mansa's pain.

She heard coughing and saw another face appear in the periphery of her vision. Mansa squinted but it took a while for her to realise who it was.

"Rupa?" she asked. Rupa covered her mouth with her hand and turned away coughing. Once the burst had finished she turned back to greet Mansa with a raised hand, the other hand held across her chest.

"You gave us a scare. We didn't think we were going to get you out," Rupa said before turning away to cough again.

"What happened?" Mansa asked once the fit finished, still clinging on to Anitha's hand, afraid that if she let go she would lose her again.

"You were in the tree, probably trying to hide from the riots. Then *this* one," she said, putting an arm around Anitha's shoulders and squeezing her, "was there trying to haul you out. Long story short, between her and Ben we managed to get you out and back here." Mansa glanced around to figure out where *here* was. The van! It was the van she recognised. She realised she was laid out on one of the back seats where she had been interviewed.

"Thank you," she whispered, humbled. Rupa smiled.

"Now you need to rest, we all do. It's been some day." With that, Rupa resumed coughing and turned away. Mansa felt Anitha's tiny hand still in hers and squeezed her slender fingers. Anitha returned the squeeze and within seconds her auntie was asleep again.

Chapter 33

Anitha and Rupa

Anitha sat on the dusty ground outside the van. In her hand she held a small stone that she idly turned between her fingers. She was exhausted but she couldn't sleep. Too many thoughts ruined her dreams. As she closed her eyes the face of Prabu would appear, pleading, asking her to help him. She reached out, but her arms were never long enough to get to him. He would be falling, slipping away and there was nothing that she could do.

She dreamt of her friend Javali. They would be happily playing on the rope by the stream, when suddenly the men would come out of the forest and drag Javali away. She tried to stop them but would wake up with Javali's screams in her head.

Then she would find herself in the back of the car. The body of Mr Kalluri was there next to her and in her hands she held the knife that had killed him. Blood ran over its golden handle and dripped on to her arms. In her panic she wiped her bloodied hands on her sari, but the handprints came alive, pointing and accusing her. The men came after her and chased her through the forest, the silver-haired man at the front shouting at the others to catch her. Suddenly he changed from being a man into a ball of flames, burning up everything around him as he got closer and closer to her. She would awake screaming, her cheeks burning like the fire which had chased her.

Would the men still be looking for her? Was she putting them all in trouble by being here? She had to tell them what she had seen, but would they believe her? Would the camera people have helped her if they knew everything she had seen and done? *She* was the one who had caused all the trouble.

The sun was beginning to rise and she was able to see the whole village from up here. She had never travelled this far before, never been further than the woods with Javali, but as she sat on the top of the hill she could see the dark smoke still lazily making its way into the sky. The temple was now just a big black pile of rubble, crumbled bricks scattered on the ground where it had once stood. The proud banyan tree was now like a giant shadow, reduced to blackened branches surrounded by ash. Dotted about she could see people scurrying around, looking like ants from her vantage point up here. Most of the ground was black and she could see dark spots all over the village where huts had caught fire. The ground in front of the temple ruins was surrounded by lots of police cars and she could see people gathered around the cars, running back and forth between them. There was a huge black streak cutting through the trees that she had run through last night, with a faint orange glow still spreading outwards as men from the village ran around trying to stop it.

From up here she could raise up a hand and cover the whole village. She could pretend none of the events had ever happened. She could imagine everything was fine and she could walk home to see Prabu alive and well again.

It had all gone though. Everything she had once known.

Her whole life. What would happen to her now? Even her own mother didn't want her anymore.

She wished that her auntie would look after her but she would say the same as her mother when she knew all that she had done. If it wasn't for her, Prabu would be here, alive and well.

The men would be looking for her too. Maybe it was best to just walk off now and hope no-one ever found her. She was too tired to move though and she didn't have anywhere to hide anyway. Everywhere she once knew was gone, and up here was completely new to her. As soon as they had got to the van yesterday, the nice man who had helped her and her auntie began driving as quickly as he could away from the village. He had driven so quickly she was scared they would hit something. Up and up they had climbed, leaving the fire and the crowds behind them. Every turn in the road the noise grew quieter and quieter until it seemed like it was just a distant dream from another time.

They had eventually stopped here, near the top of a big hill. The man looked too tired to keep driving, his eyes were barely open and a few times the van almost disappeared off the road so Rupa told him to pull over before he killed them all and did Chaudhury's job for him. Anitha was just glad they didn't have to go any further. They had parked the van away from the road, hidden slightly among the trees.

When they stopped, her auntie had woken up and they had made sure she was alright, then they all found a space in the van to sleep. She didn't think anyone was sleeping very much though. She kept hearing coughing and groans of pain from everywhere in the van. She imagined it's what it sounded like in a hospital, with all of the ill people kept in one room.

Anitha stayed by her auntie's side, holding her hand until she was fast asleep. She watched her auntie's eyes twitching as she mumbled to herself, repeating Anitha's name over and over. After a short time Anitha felt her own eyes closing, and the nightmares began as she flitted in and out of consciousness. Gently removing her hand from her auntie's she had crept outside to escape the dark memories sleep returned to her.

Anitha drew her knees up to her chest, hugging them close for comfort. As soon as they woke up she would tell them what she had seen in the car. If they wanted to leave her, she would understand. She didn't want to cause them trouble as she had for everyone else.

The door to the van slowly creaked open. Rupa stepped out, her eyes still red and puffy as she stretched her arms, wincing as she did so. Her face was serious as she surveyed the smouldering village in the valley, until she spotted Anitha. As she did, her eyes softened and she offered a smile.

"Hey Anitha," she said as cheerily as she possibly could, before coughing into her sleeve. Rupa squatted down next to her in the dirt. "How are you holding up? You OK?" she asked. Anitha looked down at the ground not wanting to meet her eye. She shrugged her shoulders.

"What is it?" Rupa asked. Still looking at the ground Anitha waited for a moment, then replied, "Before the fire, I saw something terrible and I don't know what to do."

Chapter 34

Mansa and Anitha

It was well after sunrise when Mansa left the van. Her head was still pounding and was now covered with a fresh bandage, the crisp white material smudged by Ben's sooty fingerprints where he had applied it. Her lungs still felt like they had been dragged through broken glass, every single breath causing a million tiny cuts. The pain increased as she stood, but she needed fresh air and to escape the confines of the van for a few minutes. Besides, she had to speak with Anitha.

Mansa tottered timidly down the steps of the van onto the arid ground before her. Anitha was sitting a little distance away, rolling a stone in her hands as she watched it intently. Mansa came and sat next to her, the pain from every movement biting at her skull. Anitha looked up at her wide-eyed, fear on her face.

"It's OK," Mansa said, "Rupa told me everything." Anitha's eyes were full of terror as she scanned Mansa's face for a reaction. "I'm so sorry you had to go through all that." She said, placing a comforting arm around Anitha's trembling shoulders. "This should never have happened to you, any of it. You're safe now though." Anitha sat rigidly, waiting for her auntie to shout and send her away for what had happened, but Mansa just held her under her arm as she gazed into the distance. Slowly Anitha melted in her auntie's embrace, so grateful to feel wanted.

After a few moments of silence, Mansa stretched out a

hand and pointed to the blackened corpse of the village far below them.

"Your mother and I used to play in those woods you know, except back then they covered as far as the eye could see. As the village has got bigger, more of the woods have gone. She would hide and then I would try to find her, but we would never go far. We were too scared. We never went very far from home. When we were small we would play in there for hours on end, sometimes with the other girls from the village, sometimes just the two of us. I liked it best when it was only us though. After, we would sometimes skip home, hand in hand."

Anitha had never heard any of this. Her mother had hardly ever spoken of their auntie, let alone of them when they were little. She couldn't imagine her mother as a child, playing games and having fun. Fascinated, she sat and listened.

"Our mother was a Jogini, so often we would work most of the day sweeping the temple steps. We didn't know who our father was. Whenever we asked she would point to the temple and tell us Yellamma was our mother and our father. She told us that when we became older, your mother would become a Jogini too, to continue the tradition. She was told that she would bring blessings to the whole village." Mansa's lips tightened as her jaw clenched. She stared at the blackened remains of the temple as she spoke. "One day we were out in woods and your mother fell over and hurt herself. I went back home to tell our mother what had happened, but as I ran into the hut I saw her on the floor, the priest naked on top of her. I stood there, shocked, not able to say anything until my mother looked up and saw me. She cursed at me, telling me to leave, so I did. I ran from there, all the way to the woods where I sat and tried to figure out what had been happening. Your mother asked what was wrong, what I had seen, but I couldn't tell her. I felt such shame and wanted to protect her from it." Mansa stopped and coughed, then wiped her mouth with her sari.

"After that, my naivety was gone. I began to understand the frequent visits of men to our house. I knew where mother's bruises came from and why on certain days she couldn't leave our hut to perform her duties at the temple. She would drink a lot to help her deal with the pain and then get angry at us." Mansa sighed, looking back at Anitha. "The time came for your mother to be dedicated. She was still oblivious to all that it meant to become a Jogini and began to grow excited at this 'honour' she was to receive. Knowing what was to happen, I pleaded with our mother to stop it. My little sister couldn't face the same things as mother had. She looked at me, her eyes heavy, and said, 'You speak like we have a choice. We are Dalits. There is no choice, this is already spoken. We need the blessings it will bring.' I argued and pleaded with her but it was no good, so eventually, after many tears, I offered to take her place. After much thought she agreed and I was dedicated as a Jogini." Mansa sighed.

"To begin with, your mother was furious I had taken this from her. She thought it was her right, that it would make her special, but after she understood what was being done to me, she gladly accepted her role and we never spoke of it again. In fact, we never spoke much at all after that. We stopped playing after the dedication. There was always work to do and

I felt a darkness so overwhelming inside of me that I rarely spoke to anyone, let alone laughed anymore. I never felt like playing and your mother stopped asking."

"In time, your mother was married to a man in the village. He was quite handsome and a bit older than she was, and she had to move to live with his family, leaving me and our mother at home. She almost seemed relieved when she first left as it meant she no longer had to pretend not to see the pain I was in. The unspoken words between us were easily left when we weren't living in the same hut.

I would visit her from time to time and she seemed happy enough. However, more than anything she wanted a boy to please her husband, but after a number of years she was still childless. People in the village were talking, saying that maybe she was unable to conceive. Every night she cried herself to sleep, praying to Yellamma for a child. Her husband would shout at her and ask why he was working so hard in the cotton fields if there was no son to carry on his name. She never told me how sad it made her, but I could see it on her face. Every day she worried.

However, I had worries of my own. It had been three months since my bleed and I was sure that I had become pregnant by one of the *visitors* in the night. I knew that if I had a girl, from the moment she was born the expectation of the village would be upon her to continue the tradition and to become a Jogini; there would be no escaping it. After years of living through that pain, I couldn't have a child and allow them to face the same trauma and heartache. So I did what I thought was best." Anitha felt Mansa's body stiffen next to her. Again, Mansa looked away into the distance, unable to make eye contact. She stopped for a moment, and Anitha was unsure if she was going to continue. After a deep sigh she went on.

"A relative in Chennai was very ill so Mother sent us to pay the respect of our family as she was not well enough to travel herself. The opportunity seemed too good. As we waited at the station, your mother moaned to me of how desperately she wanted to have a baby. I told her I was pregnant and was terrified for the child's future, having to live as a Jogini." Mansa lifted her sari and wiped a tear that ran from down the side of her face. As she continued her voice choked while she fought back the tears. "We made a plan. No-one in Chennai knew us well, so we introduced ourselves each as the other. We looked fairly similar so no-one suspected a thing. As I grew with child we were told to stay so that I could be looked after until the child was born. In Chennai there was a hospital and we were well taken care of. When we got back, your mother took the child, promising to look after it and love it as her own and I went back to the temple." With that she broke down covering her face with both hands. Anitha sat stunned, trying to figure out if it meant what she thought it did. Mansa looked up at her through the tears. "That child was you Anitha. You were mine." She sobbed uncontrollably, rocking back and forth as she said *sorry* over and over. Anitha sat open-mouthed, trying to comprehend what she had heard. She tentatively placed her arms around Mansa, then hugged her as she felt her trembling beneath her arms.

"It's ok," Anitha responded softly, completely bemused by

what she had just heard. After a few moments Mansa regained her composure.

"I couldn't let them do that to you. When you were born I held you here in my hands," she said motioning to her palms. "I couldn't let something so terrible happen to someone so beautiful. It was the only way I could think of. I have never been able to forgive myself though. After I gave you away the blackness all but consumed me. Every time I saw you it was like a thorn pricking my heart. I thought it was best if I just went, so I planned to take my life. I couldn't live with what I had done." Anitha took her gently by the hand.

"What happened then?"

"One day, before a Jatara, a group of ladies arrived in the village. They were telling girls about their rights, that it was *illegal* to dedicate them. I came to listen and heard them talking about a new life, away from the temple. We were offered a job, somewhere to live, dignity and freedom. The girls listened, but when the village elders came they were too scared. They were told of the shame they would bring to their family by leaving, told it was their duty to Yellamma and that they would bring curses on those they loved if they left. I went home too, but something there touched me. I wanted that new life, away from my life as a Jogini. The ladies were chased away, but a few months later they returned before another Jatara, again telling girls of their rights and the possibility of a new life. Some listened, but most were too scared. I knew that it was my time to go. I asked them to take me and they did. I longed to take you with me, but everyone thought that you were my sister's child and I couldn't destroy her and her marriage by taking you from her. I made my sister promise to look after you, and treat you as her own daughter. I also promised to send money for you every month. I cried until there were no tears in the world left at having to leave, but hoped it would be the best for you."

She took Anitha's face in her hands. "I never should have left you. I hope one day you can forgive me." Anitha looked at her, then bent low, touching her mother's feet as a sign of respect. Mansa caught her by the arms, bending down with her.

"Stop! Please, I don't deserve it. Not after all that I have done to you."

"You did what you thought was right. There is nothing to forgive," Anitha said.

Mansa swept her up in her arms. "Thank you! I will never let you go again!" she promised.

Standing on the mountain, they embraced each other as they looked at the ashes of the village still smoking in the valley below.

Chapter 35

Rupa, Anitha and Mansa

Rupa finished telling the boys all that Anitha had revealed to her about the death of Chaudhury. Ben let out a low whistle as he shook his head.

"That's cold man. This guy is ruthless. Didn't Chaudhury help get him in power into the first place? How could he just kill his partner?"

"That need for power. He felt threatened he was going to lose it and he did what he thought he had to keep it." Stuart said. He sat with his legs resting on the seats and his arm across his chest in the homemade sling Ben had created for him from an old t-shirt and a few pins. Below him were as many cushions as possible to ease the pain of his back. "Someone like that won't stop till they've got it all, I guess."

"That and his hatred of the Dalits mentioned in the newspaper articles. You saw what happened last night, that sort of riot can't be a one-off spark. He must have been feeding that hatred for a while. You can see how he was blaming Kalluri for the hanging and everything else going on to make sure he was as hated by the Dalits as he was. The thought of Kalluri leaving him and jumping into bed with the Dalit Freedom Party must have repulsed him." Rupa added.

"So by killing Kalluri, Chaudhury gets power, and the sympathy of all the upper castes who fear what has happened, while at the same time making the Dalit Freedom Party and anyone associated with them reviled by everyone else.

Shrewd, very shrewd," Stuart said.

"Shrewd is one word for him. I can think of something a lot better though," Ben said.

"So what happens now then?" Stuart asked, looking at Rupa.

"First up, we are getting you straight to a hospital." She stopped and broke into a coughing fit. Ben looked around then handed her a warm, half-drunk bottle of water. She nodded thanks at him. "To be honest, I think we could all do with a good check-up. Last night can't have done any of us any favours."

"But I mean everything else. The village is pretty much toast, this Chaudhury has managed to destroy it and stir up some pretty crazy riots. He stands to take power for the whole state and the girl who knows the truth of everything he has done is sitting outside our van. He's not going to just let her walk away is he?"

"Like you said Stuart, the village is toast. Who knows how many were lost in the fire and the fighting? The whole temple was destroyed, he'll probably just assume that she was caught in the fire if she can't be found." Ben and Stuart exchanged nervous looks and Rupa's own doubts were evident through her facade of nonchalance.

"But what if he doesn't just *assume*? He doesn't strike me as the kind of guy to just let things go, know what I mean?" Ben said. "We've just heard what he did to his own partner. Not being funny, but I'm pretty sure that a lot of the police here are probably going to ask 'how high' if he tells them to jump. He craves the power, what's to say he won't have all of them out looking? What's to say she, and us, are going to be safe?" They sat silently for a moment before a faint smile crossed Stuart's lips. "The need for power. That's what." Ben looked at him completely baffled.

"We've talked about the whole power trip thing man. We're talking about him coming after *Anitha* now. Has that blow to the arm affected your head?"

"No, I mean he sees Anitha as weak, a small girl. Who would believe a single word that she could say? The whole hanging thing, no-one listened to the girl. She's so far off his radar she probably doesn't even register. Also, he's told everyone it was a big group of Dalits who killed Kalluri. It might raise some questions if he gets too worked up about *her*."

Ben looked at Rupa who shrugged then coughed. "You might have a point. That's a risk I'm not too willing to take though. We need to get moving as far from here as quickly as we can. Agreed?" Stuart and Ben both nodded. "Ben, are you well enough to drive? Stuart, you can take more painkillers and get some rest."

"Sounds like a plan, Batman," Stuart said, and then giggled.

"Man you really need some sleep!" Ben said, standing. He looked at Rupa. "The girl, Anitha," he began, pausing to find the right words. "Would she speak? I mean, I know no-one here might listen to her, but if she's got a camera on her seems like a lot more people might take notice. That could blow this whole thing out of the water."

"Ben, not now," Rupa said, shaking her head. He took off

his hat and held his hands out to show mock defence.

"Hey, I'm just asking the question I'm pretty sure we are all thinking."

"I know, but after everything she has been through, I can't ask her to do it. Mansa begged that I don't ask her. As long as her face doesn't show up on some TV screen, then they can pretend that she died in the fire and start a quiet life together back at the factory. This is probably her only shot at freedom."

Ben sighed. "Fair enough, I know it makes sense. There's got to be some way of telling what Anitha saw though without putting her in danger."

"Could we not blank her face?" Stuart asked. "It would give some privacy?"

"I thought about that, but Chaudhury is going to know straight away when he hears what she says. I don't think Mansa would go for it," Rupa said.

"There's got to be something we could do," Ben said.

Slowly the door creaked open and Mansa and Anitha timidly entered, both faces streaked with tears. Anitha looked at Rupa, her face intent.

"I have decided I want to speak. I must say what I saw."

Epilogue

It was only midday, but the whirr of the machines had ceased in the factory as the ladies gathered around the black and white TV on the highest shelf in Anna Ma'am's small office. They all crammed in, the walls lined with ladies standing while others peered over their shoulders for a better view. In the centre, more ladies sat on the floor, piles of old cloth serving as cushions. At the front of the crowd Anitha sat in a new red salwar kameez, her hair hanging behind her in a single plait. She rested her head on the shoulder of Mansa, who sat beaming with pride.

"Anna Ma'am, maybe Amir Khan can come and visit soon now that we have our own celebrity?" Joshna shouted excitedly across the room. The other ladies laughed while a small group began to recite one of his dance routines before slapping each other on the arms and giggling.

"We could make a special suit for his next film!" another shouted.

"I would much rather Hrithik Roshan came. He is far more handsome. I could measure him for his suit!" More giggles followed as one of the ladies pretended to swoon and another caught her.

"Quiet now!" an older lady shouted sternly as the newsreader appeared outside a police station. The ladies all hushed each other, then turned eagerly to the crackly screen. The reporter was speaking animatedly, struggling to be heard over the cries of the crowd behind her. Many carried placards while others blew whistles. A line of police struggled to keep them all back as a white van arrived, driving slowly through the mayhem, rocks bouncing off its bonnet and sides.

"We can see the one time leader of the BSP, Mr Chaudhury, now being driven into the police station to begin his jail sentence for several counts, including inciting violence and the murder of his long-time associate and partner Chief Minister Kalluri," she shouted, a finger in one ear to block out the noise. The camera swooped past her, catching sight of Chaudhury in handcuffs being led from the van, attempting to cover his face as he was led up the steps flanked by police officers. They had formed a shield around him as they made their way to the station. The crowd had reached a frenzy at this point, waving their placards demanding for him to be hanged as they animatedly booed and jeered. The newsreader waited for him to disappear inside, before shouting to be heard over the ruckus.

"The police were alerted to Chaudhury's involvement in the murder through the international attention created by the recent documentary broadcast worldwide 'Blessed, Bound and Broken' which featured an interview with a Jogini who claimed to have seen Chief Minister Kalluri being stabbed by Mr Chaudhury." At this, the women all cheered, Anitha bashfully looking at the screen. Those near enough reached over and patted her on the back as Mansa squeezed her hand. The screen changed to footage of Anitha recorded on the edge of a wood. Her hair was tangled and her sari ripped, Rupa having staged the scene a few nights later to look like it was shot before the fire on the night of the Jatara.

She spoke nervously, her eyes flicking from the screen

and then to Rupa behind the camera. "Chief Minister Kalluri spoke of joining together with the Dalit Freedom Party and finishing his time with Mr Chaudhury. Mr Chaudhury got so angry that he grabbed him around the neck, and tried to choke him with his belt. He then stabbed him repeatedly with Chief Minister Kalluri's own knife until the life had disappeared from him. I was so scared that he was then going to hurt me."

The screen cut back to the reporter who continued, "Sadly, the Jogini who was interviewed tragically lost her life in the fire which destroyed the temple as well as much of the village of Agnipatnam on the very night of this interview. We commend her on her bravery for speaking out. Her story was backed up by the discovery of papers in the back of the Chief Minister's car signed between him and Mr Rani, the leader of the Dalit Freedom Party, speaking of this agreement. Further police investigations went on to show that the marking around Chief Minister Kalluri's neck was consistent with her claims, as well as the recovery of the knife still within the car which has shown finger prints matching Mr Chaudhury. This conclusive evidence has led to the arrest with trial to follow for Mr Chaudhury. We will be following the trial with interest. This is Shobu Myal reporting from Hyderabad," she said, the crowd continuing to scream in the background.

With that, all of the women burst into applause, whooping and cheering as they held Anitha's hands in the air, a nervous smile covering her face. Question after question was fired at her until Anna Ma'am began to usher all the ladies back to work. "I think Anitha has had more than enough questions for one day." She came up and squeezed Anitha's hand.

"We are all so proud of you for your courage," she said, before smiling and walking out of the office, leaving her alone with Mansa.

"Are you OK?" Mansa asked Anitha, noticing how tired she looked. Anitha nodded.

"It was strange, seeing the video with me in it, then they said I was thought to be dead in the fire. It made me shiver thinking what might have happened." Mansa nodded in sympathy. "It feels like it's only since the fire that I have been alive though. Thank you for coming back for me, mum." Mansa looked at her, overwhelmed at being called mum for the first time in her life.

"I shouldn't have left you once. I never will again," Mansa said putting an arm around her daughter's shoulders as they walked out of the office.

Around them machines heated up as the women finished their chai and got back to work. The rhythmic hum of the machines was interspersed with the sound of chatter and laughter.

It was a strange new sound, but it was the sound of home.

Can you help?

While the story of Blessed, Bound and Broken is purely fictional, the issues raised are all too real. Thankfully there are charities doing amazing things to fight against many of the injustices mentioned in the novel. Those listed below are all close to my heart, and I have been blessed to visit and see the work of most of them first hand. Please visit their websites to find out about the great things they are doing and how you can get involved!

Life Association

My wife and I volunteered for a year with Life Association in Andhra Pradesh. While there we worked in their orphanage school which provides a home and education for Dalit children. We taught English, art and crafts, sport and much more alongside local staff. The orphanage school helps give an opportunity to children who would otherwise have very limited options.

Life Association have a number of other projects which work with people from the Dalit caste, who often face immense persecution. One of these projects works in the Dharavi slum in Mumbai with potters who create amazing handmade candles as well as well a range of spice boxes and soaps (which make beautiful presents!)

You can find out more at www.lifeassociation.org.uk

Dalit Freedom Network

The inspiration behind Blessed, Bound and Broken came from my visit to Dalit Freedom Network's Indian partners in Andhra Pradesh. That is where I heard about the Joginis and felt compelled to raise awareness of the dedications taking place.

The Jogini system of ritual sex slavery still exists in the Indian state of Telangana and elsewhere. In 2015, the Jogini Commission estimated there are around 80,000 Joginis today. Dalit Freedom Network UK's partner organisation, Pratigya India, is one of the few organisations working directly on the Jogini issue. They work in 100 villages, home to over 1,700 Joginis. During the last 3 to 4 years Pratigya has stopped 20 dedications, and prevented dozens more girls from being forced into ritual sex slavery.

Pratigya empowers Joginis by helping them access government benefits and schemes, and by working with local officials, for example, to give their children access to education. In addition to this Prevention and Awareness Programme, Pratigya help Joginis to set up microbusinesses through small grants and LAMP self help groups. These not only help provide a livelihood, but also restores their dignity.

The Kapade Akka health initiative provides basic health education and access to diagnosis and treatment through community health workers. Pratigya also runs a children's shelter primarily for girls most at risk of being dedicated. The children are in a caring environment, with basic healthcare, access to counseling and places in a good quality school.

Find out more about the work of Dalit Freedom Network UK at www.dfn.org.uk and how you can help Free A Woman at www.dfn.org.uk/freeawoman

FREE A CHILD, FREE A WOMAN, FREE A COMMUNITY

Freeset

While in Kolkata, my wife and I visited the factory of Freeset and were amazed by their brilliant work. Here's a bit about them.

Freeset is a fair trade business offering employment to women trapped in Kolkata's sex trade. We make quality jute bags and organic cotton t-shirts, but our business is freedom!

We would like to see the 10,000 sex workers in our neighborhood empowered with the choice of leaving a profession they never chose in the first place.

Have a look at our website to see more of what we do and to order our products www.freesetglobal.com/

Hagar

Hagar is an international organization dedicated to the protection, recovery and community integration of survivors of human rights abuse; particularly human tracking, gender based violence and torture. We do whatever it takes for as long as it takes to restore life in all its fullness, and partner with the not for profit, government and for profit sectors to achieve our mission.

We believe in the impossible. Because we have seen that when we care for women and children until they can care for themselves. When we give them the freedom to think about the future. When we help them find jobs, and families and help them reunite with society again, that miracles happen.

Visit www.hagarinternational.org/united-kingdom/ and also www.facebook.com/HagarUK

Also by David Skivington...

Scar Tissue

ISBN 978-1-906377-68-7

In a single phone call, Rachel's entire life unravels. Transported to a dingy basement in Kolkata to identify the body of her murdered husband she has no explanation for his presence in India.

As she searches for answers about who the man she married really was she finds his death surrounded by allegations of drug smuggling, child trafficking and murder.

Unsure of what is true and who she can trust, Rachel has no idea of the danger her husband's hidden life has put her in.

'...Scar Tissue is a shockingly authentic portrayal of sex trafficking. In addition to being an engaging story this book is a timely reminder that the tentacles of modern day slavery reach into every country and into every community.
Scar Tissue will impact every reader and serves as an invitation to join the fight to set people free.'

Daniel Walker -
Author of God in a Brothel and founder of Nvader